TIGHTROPE

Alone in his squalid bed-sitter, Johnny Baxter thought about the mysterious 'phone call he had just taken. Maybe his run of bad luck was about to change; the man had offered him money to do a simple job, and Johnny wasn't going to question too closely what it might entail—he was down to his last few pounds. But 24 hours later, Johnny found that the caller had left him with a packet of diamonds and £6,000 in cash— plus a whole lot of problems.

TIGHTROPE

James Grant

A Lythway Book

CHIVERS PRESS
BATH

First published in Great Britain 1979
by
Frederick Muller Limited
This Large Print edition published by
Chivers Press
by arrangement with Frederick Muller Limited
1983

ISBN 0 85119 908 9

British Library Cataloguing in Publication Data

Grant, James
　　Tightrope.—Large print ed.—
　　(A Lythway book)
　　Rn : Bruce Crowther　　　　I. Title
　　823′.914[F]　　　　PR6053.R657

　　ISBN 0–85119–908–9

The city in which this novel is set is real, as are certain streets, Public Buildings, public houses and the like. It is however a work of fiction and except for the names of certain personalities from the world of music, all characters are imaginary.

TIGHTROPE

CHAPTER ONE

It was a cold, wet, miserable evening and it suited the mood I'd been in since I woke up that morning. Not that the day was all that different to most other days. I still had the head cold I'd been nursing for the past three weeks; my leg still ached like hell whether I sat down, stood up or walked about—a result of breaking it in four places a few months before, and an effect the doctors at the hospital kept assuring me would wear off—which meant that the only time it didn't ache was when I was in bed; I was still out of work and I was still broke, the Welfare State having a blind spot where several million people like me, the self-employed, are concerned. What made this day just a little bit worse than all the others was that it was my birthday. I don't know why being thirty-six was any worse than being thirty-five, but it was.

I parked the car in a side street along with about a hundred others. I wondered if the people who lived in the street felt the same way about motorists as I did when people parked outside the house where I had my room. I reckoned they probably did, so I showed my appreciation of their problem by closing the door quietly.

I walked the hundred yards or so along the

main road to the traffic lights. A few cars swished past on the wet road, more heading out of town than in. I felt like joining them, the prospect of spending the winter there didn't have any appeal; no appeal at all.

Not that I had very much against the place; after all, one big city is very much like any other, only this one, Hull, seemed to have a peculiar, defeated air all its own. In my state of mind a winter there would be like giving a loaded gun to a man with suicidal tendencies.

I shrugged my shoulders at the weather, turned my back on the wet road and went into the pub. Maybe the man I was meeting there would help break my run of bad luck and provide me with enough readies to get me out of the city for a few months. It didn't seem very likely but I pretended it was. After all it was my birthday, maybe somebody up there had a note to that effect and was about to ensure I got a present to celebrate the event.

Considering the weather, the fact that it was only eight o'clock and it was Tuesday, there was a large crowd inside. Most of them young with long hair, jeans and thick sweaters and the proud possessors of slightly too-loud voices. It was reasonable to assume that they were students, the university was less than half a mile away and the Haworth Arms was one of the nearest pubs. I pushed my way to the bar and ordered a pint of bitter. Beer isn't my drink, least of all when I have a head cold but my finances didn't run to scotch. I fought my way back out of the crush, standing on a few toes in the process. I got dirty looks from a couple of bearded wonders but ignored them. I was bigger than they were.

I went up the stairs to the concert room and sat alone at a small round table. Its plastic laminated top showed signs of having been tested frequently for its resistance to cigarette burns. It had failed.

A few other people were already there, others followed me in and slowly the room began to fill up. Nobody joined me at my little table.

Although my hair was long and I was dressed in casual trousers and a leather jacket, already showing its age, it was obvious I wasn't their kind. Too old I expect. Too old at thirty-six. Christ!

The band had started unpacking their instruments. I watched them for something to look at other than the students, I was beginning to resent them for no apparent reason. I realised I knew the leader of the band by sight, he worked for the Social Security people by day and I'd had one or two hassles with him in the past, but I hadn't known he was a jazz musician. I felt a tiny bit less antagonistic towards him. He opened up a scuffed, rexine-covered case and took out a cornet that looked as if it had seen recent service as a pot-plant holder. He pointed

3

it at the floor and experimentally blew a hatful of bum notes. Somebody at the back of the room cheered, apparently without irony. The cornet-player looked pleased with his reception and tried again. He didn't do any better that time either and I decided I had been premature in diminishing my antagonism.

Behind him the rest of the band were trying out various odds and ends on their instruments and I experienced a sinking feeling that the day that had started badly wasn't going to end very brightly either.

I picked up my glass and looked at its contents. Like some wines it didn't appear to travel well, at least the journey up the stairs hadn't done a lot for it and the froth had degenerated into a few zestless bubbles. I stood it down again and wondered why my unknown caller of that afternoon had chosen this place, of all the pubs in town, for a meeting and why in the concert room. Maybe he had a thing about traditional jazz bands.

The call had come just as I was closing the door to my one room on the top floor of a three-storey house in Park Street. Once upon a time, maybe a hundred years ago, it had been the home of a prosperous Victorian and the street had been select. Now it was the home of various impoverished transients like me and select it very definitely was not. The telephone was a coin-operated instrument on the second-floor landing and as I was the only one around at that time of day, the other tenants being out collecting their dole money or picking the losers in the local betting shop, I answered it.

'I want to talk to Johnny Baxter,' the voice had said. It was a deep, dark voice with an American accent.

'Who shall I say wants him?' I asked, pitching my voice an octave higher than usual.

'Just get him,' the voice said with an air of finality that suggested its owner wasn't accustomed to playing games.

I waited a moment or two, using the time to consider the possibilities. As far as I was aware I didn't owe money to any Americans and as I hadn't done anything to feel guilty about I decided I had nothing to lose talking to the man.

'This is Baxter,' I said in my normal voice. 'Who are you and what do you want?'

'I'm told you could do with earning some money,' he said, ignoring my questions.

'That's always possible.'

That was when he told me where and when to meet him and before I had time to ask any more questions he hung up on me.

I replaced the receiver and almost at once the telephone rang again.

'Johnny?' I didn't have any trouble with identification that time. My ex-wife's accent is pure Geordie and shrill with it.

'Yes,' I said. I didn't need to ask what she

5

wanted, she always wanted the same thing and I leaned against the wall and switched off part of my brain.

'You haven't sent me any money for over a month,' she said. It was true, I hadn't. There was a good reason for my omission and I thought about telling her what it was but decided against it. For one thing she wouldn't believe me and for another I didn't like the idea of grovelling to Sandra.

We had married before either of us were old enough to know better, I was twenty and she was about a year and a half younger. Before the year was out we both knew we'd made a mistake but by then there was an obstacle to us going our separate ways, a baby, a girl we called Susie and who we tried to use as glue. We stayed together and argued and fought and then, gradually, the arguments and fights lessened, not because our relationship improved but simply because it no longer seemed worth the effort the fighting took. We had done what millions of other couples did, we'd drifted into indifference.

Things stayed that way until we'd been married about five years and then some of my mates got into serious bother with the law. Previously I had been encouraged by lack of work, and corresponding lack of money, to run with a small gang of tearaways for a few months. We pulled a few little jobs, nothing spectacular, in fact apart from adding to the crime statistics, they did very little else. Certainly the loot, when divided by four, sometimes five, did nothing to off-set the slightly shattering effect it had on my nerves. I came to the conclusion that I wasn't cut out for a life of crime and opted out. The rest of the gang sneered briefly and then went out and did another job, netting a couple of thousand pounds. I was out of my mind with anger and jealousy for about three days. That was how long it took the law to nail them.

The police questioned me, of course, but nothing came of it, except that my wife left me. She left with tears and aggravation plus a couple of minor skirmishes with her man-hating mother and that was that. I made one or two gestures towards reconciliation but my heart wasn't in it and, anyway, she wasn't the slightest bit receptive. When she sued for divorce I let it all happen without a struggle. It was a pity about little Susie but any regrets I felt over that particular loss also faded over the following few years as my daughter's attitude towards me slowly changed, no doubt a direct result of Sandra putting the boot in as far as Daddy was concerned at every possible opportunity.

I turned back in to Sandra's voice. She was busy telling me some highly complicated tale about new clothes being wanted for Susie. I didn't think it would do much good to point out that I could do with something to keep the rain out myself.

'Okay,' I interrupted. 'I'll do what I can.'

'When?' she asked, reversing the usual sequence of her two unfailing questions.

'As soon as I can. Next week at the latest.'

'Alright,' she said, sulkily. 'See that you don't forget.'

I waited for her to ask how much I would send, the other of her two inevitable questions. I was supposed to send a fixed amount, fixed by the court that is, not by reality. Neither Sandra nor I had ever pretended the sum was anything other than a general guideline. Regular payments needed a regular income, something I never had and never looked like getting.

I realised she had hung up without asking the question. It seemed an unusual omission and I wondered briefly if she had grown soft in the four or five months that had elapsed since I'd last talked to her. I shrugged off the thought, there didn't seem much chance of that, maybe she had something else on her mind.

Sitting there, in the Haworth Arms, not drinking my beer and watching the musicians talking earnestly amongst themselves, I hoped my other caller would turn up with a reasonable proposition. I didn't need to take out my wallet to know that, unless something turned up by the weekend, it wouldn't be just Sandra who would be whistling for money, the landlord too would have to wait for his rent. Not for the first time either, but as he didn't come round too often, in case he got waylaid with demands for unimportant matters like sorting out the plumbing or replacing broken windows, he hadn't yet made any threatening noises.

I was faced with the unavoidable conclusion that while I'd been in worse financial binds than this one, my present state was bidding for a prize as one of the lowest points of my life. Not that I have anyone to blame but myself. I don't mean for being unable to work at the moment, that was the result of an accident and some broken bones, but there was no excuse for being broke. When I was working I earned good money and as most of it was paid in cash the taxman didn't see a lot of it. Unfortunately, that also meant I couldn't risk putting it in the bank and as I always feel nervous when I have a lot of money on me, I took the easy way out and spent it as I earned it. That meant that if the proverbial rainy day came along there was very little to keep me afloat.

That rainy day had come along in the middle of July when I was one of a small team erecting a steel-framed dutch barn on a farm in Lincolnshire. It was an easy, straight-forward job, one I'd done a hundred times before. Only this time something went wrong. Instead of the steel joists being painted with red-oxide some idiot had painted them with red-lead, not the kind of thing that goes down very well on farms, and as it had been painted only the day before it still hadn't hardened. My foot slipped and down I went. I wasn't very high, about twenty feet, but I fell badly. I suppose I could've come out of it a lot worse than I did but, as it was, I broke my left leg in four places, three of them below the knee. Now, early in October, I was still unable to get about easily enough to risk going back up ladders, scaffolding or steel, the places—the only places where I could earn decent money without doing something illegal.

The band seemed to have finished their conference, the cornet-player stamped his foot in the time-honoured fashion and they lurched into an uncertain version of the *Gettysburg March*. I'd thought the cornet-player was awful but the rest of them were so bad they made him sound like Wild Bill Davison. The trombone player sounded like a refugee from a brass band, not a very good one at that; the clarinettist was having reed trouble resulting in him making a series of sounds like someone trailing a fingernail across a blackboard; the drummer had no idea about maintaining the tempo, and before they were halfway through the march had become an unruly stampede. I couldn't hear the bass-player, which was probably fortunate and the banjo-player had gone off with a tray, presumably to fetch more beer.

Eventually they staggered to a finish and began an even less inspired rendition of *Just a Closer Walk With Thee*. That was when the man

I was waiting for arrived. Even though I'd had only that one brief talk on the telephone I didn't need to be told he was the one. He looked completely out of place, but then I can't think of anywhere he would have looked at home. He was big, not exceptionally tall, maybe an inch or so over my five-eleven and not fat, but he had a chest like a barrel and his upper arms and thighs seemed to be doing their best to punch through the material of his suit. The suit was really something to see. It appeared to have been hand-made by a palsied sail-maker with things other than tailoring on his mind. The cloth, if that's what it was, would have looked more in place across the back of the Grand National winner. The suit was set off by orange-coloured brogues and a little, narrow-brimmed, green leather hat. I listened to the whisper that ran around the room beneath the strains of the band and within seconds almost everyone was looking at him.

He came straight over to me, his hands clenched into fists in front of him. They looked odd and as he came closer I saw that his fingers were covered in intricate black, blue and red tattooing. He reached the table and rested his fists on it, unwrapping them from the two glasses of whisky they were holding. He grinned at me and looked around for an empty chair. There wasn't one close by so he hooked a leg around one that was supporting the backside of a hairy individual in dirty blue denims and pulled it away. The hairy youth was one of the few people in the room who hadn't seen the big man and he jumped to his feet, spinning round, full of fight until he saw the size of the usurper of his chair. He made a hasty, and wise, decision that discretion would save his front teeth. He settled for a glare, seconded by his friends. The big man didn't notice, or if he did he didn't care. He nodded at me and the glass of whisky in front of me, picked up the other glass and swallowed half its contents.

He glanced across at the band who were fumbling their way through a quiet passage and jerked his chin in their direction. 'Fucking jungle music,' he announced in that deep, resonant voice he had used on the telephone. It reverberated around the room bringing a sudden silence to everyone but the musicians, then the clarinet-player made a few more screeching noises and the band stumbled to a halt. I risked a cautious glance in their direction and saw that the cornet-player, at least, had heard the big man's comment. He treated me to a glower that boded ill if I ever went into his office again. Not that I'd got anything from him the last time but, as you never know when you're going to need people like that, I ventured a nervous smile just to show it wasn't my fault. I didn't get a response so I turned away and looked at the big man. The face, underneath the incongruous hat, was fleshy but there was an air of hardness that suggested the easy life was something he had yet to find.

He watched me as I looked at him and then nodded at my glass of beer. 'Don't drink that piss,' he ordered, loudly. 'It'll rot your guts.'

I picked up the glass of scotch instead and sipped at it. The silence was growing hostile and I swallowed the drink uneasily. I didn't feel up to a rough-house, at least not until I was fit and ready for one.

I was relieved when the cornet-player's foot banged on the floorboards again and the band began a medium-tempo version of *Eh, Las Bas*. After a few bars, as the drummer began to race the tempo again, the audience showed the level of their musical appreciation by tapping their toes to it.

I breathed a little more easily, there seemed to be a better than even chance I would get out of there in one piece but then, again choosing a quiet passage from the band, the big man struck again. This time he finished off his scotch in one swallow, hitched himself half out of his chair and noisily broke wind. He made almost as much sound as the cornet-player, and it wasn't in B-flat either.

He grinned at me. 'Let's get out of here,' he said and stood up and marched to the door. Scrambling to my feet I followed him, trying not to meet anyone's eye and we reached the bottom

13

of the stairs without anyone taking us to task for the big man's manners. I was pleased the Haworth Arms wasn't a pub I used often, it wouldn't be safe for me to go in there for quite some time.

The big man pushed through the crowd in the downstairs bar and was outside before I was halfway through the crush. When I reached the pavement he had turned to the right and was walking, head down against the wind, towards the side street where I had parked my car. I followed him and when I turned into the street I saw that he was waiting by the nearside door of the ancient Cortina I rely on to get from place to place. That told me something about him, although I wasn't sure what it was.

I unlocked the door, slid into my seat and reached across to unlock the other door. The big man climbed in, filling all the available space at that side of the car.

'Well?' I said.

'Take me back to the city centre.'

I waited in case he was going to say anything else, like please, but it appeared that he wasn't that way inclined. I put the key in the ignition and the engine coughed vaguely before starting up with a noisy clatter from the starter, telling me where part of any money I earned from the big man would have to go.

A couple of minutes later, on the main road leading into the city centre, I tried a question.

'What's this job you want doing?'

'Later,' he said.

I hid any annoyance I felt and drove on listening to the background hiss of the Cortina's worn tyres on the wet road. After the silence had gone on long enough for me I reached out and fumbled for a cassette to put in the stereo player, one of my few remaining luxuries and which was probably worth as much as the car. More even. Then it occurred to me that if his comments in the pub were a true reflection of the big man's musical taste, I would have very little that would appeal to him.

Then I thought, the hell with it, it's my car, and I reached out again and fumbled for a cassette from the pile under the dash. Until it was in and playing I didn't know what I'd chosen, but seconds later Earl Hines and Joe Venuti were duetting on *Blues in Thirds*. By the time it finished we were in the city centre and, in the absence of any comment from the big man, I drove straight across the lights into Ferensway and slowed down, switching off the player as I did so.

'Where are we going?' I asked him.

'Beautiful,' he said.

'What?'

'That was. I prefer Hines' original with Armstrong, but that was great. I saw him once, in 1972. Overseas Press Club in New York. He had Maxine Sullivan with him. She was past her

15

best, but he wasn't. Incredible piano-player.'

'Yes.' I said. For a few seconds neither of us said anything. My mind was trying to assess the implication of the fact that this man, who had gone out of his way to make known his disapproval of jazz had recognised Earl Hines without any prompting from me.

'Here will do,' he said suddenly.

I pulled over to the kerbside, stopped and looked at him. 'Well?' I said again.

'What?'

'The job.' I was beginning to lose patience.

'Not now,' he said, opening the car door. 'Tomorrow morning, ten o'clock at the public library.' Before I had time to say anything in answer to that he had gone, the door closing behind him with a bang.

I watched him hurry along a short distance before he turned off and disappeared from my sight. I put the Cortina into gear, swung it across the road, around a traffic island, and went back towards the traffic lights which promptly turned red and made me wait before I could go through and turn to the left and head for home, aware that, unless someone had left a packet of pound notes in my letter box, the day had been even worse than usual.

I keep the car in a garage behind the house where I live. It had once been a big, roomy place, probably a stable, but somewhere along the line it had been divided into two by a timber

16

partition. The half I used was just wide enough to allow me to get the car in but the door was off-set so that once inside I couldn't open my door and had to get out by scrambling across the seat to the off-side of the car.

It was while I was performing that particular exercise, not made any easier by my left leg's stiffness, that I noticed the big man had dropped something down between the seat and the door, just below the level of the door sill. It was a small brown-paper wrapped package about the size of a paperback novel and all stuck neatly together with Sellotape. I picked it up, dropped it into the pocket of my jacket and closed the car door. I locked it and then locked the garage door reflecting that anyone who wanted to steal a car wouldn't waste his time and risk his liberty on a heap like mine. If the garage hadn't been in with the rent for the room I would have economised. As it was, there was a chance I would be doing some obligatory economising in that area sooner than I wanted.

When I reached the second floor of the house I knocked on Carole Dixon's door, but didn't get a reply. I glanced at my watch, nine-thirty was too early for her so I went on up to my room on the top floor, made some instant coffee and switched on the cassette-player. Thinking about the big man's unexpected appreciation of Earl Hines I put on a cassette of him playing solo and drank my coffee while he made *Dinah* sound a

17

hundred and one times better than Harry Akst ever dreamed it could be.

I tried to think about the job the big man might have for me the next day and then I gave up speculating on the improbable and thought about Carole instead.

She is one of those women who, at first glance, seem to have everything. Medium height, long blonde hair, straight nose, bright blue eyes and a figure that men dream of seeing. That was her trouble, too many men had seen it. She was an actress, intelligent, articulate, but she couldn't leave men alone. Somewhere along the line she'd tried drinking as a means to some kind of solution, or at least to a deadening of her problem. It hadn't worked, all that had happened was that she now had two problems: men and drink. Her reputation for both preceded her wherever she went and work had become hard to get. One night, when in a drunken stupor, the company she was with moved on and left her behind. She'd never bothered to try to catch them up.

She got occasional jobs at the Humberside Theatre which was a couple of streets away from where we lived and did other odds and ends that helped pay the rent. Recently I suspected she'd started to put her predilection for men onto a strictly cash basis. Certainly she'd begun to spend more money on clothes and a lot more on scotch. She was twenty-three and after the

18

eighth or ninth drink of the day she looked forty.

I'd met her about a year before but we hadn't spoken much, let alone gone to bed together, until about five months ago when I'd moved, after a slight disagreement with the landlord, from a room I rented in a house in what was left of Wellington Lane. I had thought a reduction in rent was called for after pointing out that I had to share the room with several small rodents and one or two hundred insects of unknown origin and unpleasant habits. The landlord hadn't agreed, using as his main argument the fact that a reduction in the rent wasn't possible when I hadn't paid it all that regularly anyway.

When I moved into the room in the house in Park Street I found Carole halfway up the stairs on my first night there, slightly drunk and very randy. It made an interesting enough house-warming and we'd gone on from there, in a casual, undemanding way. I let it all happen because, unlike a lot of drunks, she rarely, if ever, felt sorry for herself and didn't give me a lot of uncalled for junk about being a victim nor did she try to hide the fact of her addiction either. I also liked the free and easy way she had with her body and, while I was still young enough and able enough to get my share elsewhere, the convenience of having someone in the same house had a lot going for it. It saved all the pre-sex drink buying for one thing, no mean virtue

19

with someone of her capacity, and for another it meant I didn't have to crawl far when it was time to go home.

I suppose the truth of the matter was that I used her for my own convenience but I justified my actions with the thought that she used me in much the same way, if not with the same motivation.

Apart from all that, I enjoyed her company most of the time. She was bright and clever and I didn't have to use short words to make her understand what I was talking about. If circumstances, or biology or whatever it was, hadn't driven her to find some sort of solace in various compulsions then I think she would have been the right kind of woman for me to take up with on a more or less permanent basis. The trouble was, I told myself on the occasions I was being honest, if she hadn't had her compulsions she wouldn't have needed to tie herself up, however loosely, with someone like me.

Earl Hines had worked his way through seven or eight other numbers and I had replaced him with Johnny Guarnieri, who was making minor masterpieces out of a selection of Harry Warren tunes, when I heard the front door open and close with a crash. I turned off the cassette player and walked to the door and looked out to see if she was coming up alone. She was.

'Fancy a cup of coffee?' I called down as she

reached her landing.

'If that's the best you can offer.'

'In my financial state what else do you expect?'

'Come on in. I can do better than that.'

She could too. She found a bottle of scotch that was more than three-quarters full and we set about killing off the remains of my head cold.

Then we went to bed and Carole proved that whatever she had been doing earlier in the evening hadn't taken the edge off her appetite for sex. We tried several entertaining variations, including one that made me feel the way I'd felt when I fell off the building and broke my leg, then she fell asleep leaving me wide awake and undecided whether or not to go back up the stairs to my own bed. Then I began to doze and decided to stay where I was.

I woke up to the sound of heavy footsteps clumping up the stairs. They didn't sound like any of the other residents, but as the house had a fairly regular turnover of tenants that didn't mean a lot. I listened as they passed Carole's door and then proceeded up the next flight to the top floor.

I got interested. There's only one room up there apart from mine and it is used as a storeroom by the landlord until he decides to have the ceiling repaired. It seemed as if I had visitors. I thought about getting out of bed and going up to them but then I looked at my watch and changed my mind. Three o'clock in the morning isn't the time any friend of mine would turn up. I slid out of bed, went across to the window and looked down into the street. A police car was at the kerb.

I waited, listening, and then as I began to shiver I slid back into Carole's bed. Above me I could hear my visitors banging on the door. After a while they gave up and clumped noisily down the stairs again. I waited until they passed Carole's door and clattered on down towards street level before I went back to the window and watched them come out of the house and cross the pavement to their car. One of them was in uniform, a constable. Nothing very serious then. I tried to think what I'd been up to recently and came to the conclusion that I hadn't done anything to warrant a visit from the police. That conclusion didn't stop me from worrying.

I watched the car drive off and then went through into the curtained-off alcove that served as the kitchen, switched on the light and made some coffee. I felt the cold start to get to me and I went back and scraped around in the comparative darkness of the main room until I found my trousers and my jacket. I put them on, went back into the alcove and sat down to drink my coffee. As I did so I felt the package the big man had dropped in the car. I took it out of my pocket and placed it on the table in front of me and thought about him and his odd behaviour, and then I thought about the unexpected, and apparently unwarranted, visit from the law.

After a few minutes I opened a drawer or two until I found a knife. I laid it beside the package and tried to be strong-minded about other people's property. Especially big, tough-looking people like the man with the tattooed fingers. As far as I could see the brown paper was plain, ordinary, brown paper and Sellotape is Sellotape, so I wouldn't have too much trouble rewrapping it afterwards. I was still thinking over the ethical aspects of the whole thing when I slipped the point of the knife through the paper and worked it into a position where I could slit the side of the package open along its full length. It seemed my hands were less concerned with ethics than my brain.

Under the paper was a small, flat, metal box like those used to pack fancy cigarettes many years ago. I laid it on the table, opened the lid and lifted up the corner of some cotton-wool packing and then sat there holding my breath in case I woke up and the contents of the box disappeared. I'd thought, earlier, that a packet of pound notes in my letter-box was my only salvation. Fate, not usually on my side, had gone one better. A lot better. Not pound notes—diamonds.

After a while I let out my breath and made another cup of coffee and then sat down to look closely at them. I couldn't tell whether they were good stones, bad ones or merely indifferent; the only diamonds I saw regularly were on playing cards. There were thirty-one stones altogether, varying in size from the kind of thing people from my background expect to see in engagement rings up to one about as big as the nail on my middle finger.

After a while I went through into the other room and found a pile of paperback novels and took one back to measure it against the box. It fitted neatly into it and I spent another cautious ten minutes prowling among Carole's belongings until I found a small, brown paper bag that looked as if it might have held a blouse. I slit it open and cut off the seamed edge until I had a sheet about the right size. I then rewrapped the tin box and wasted more time searching for Sellotape. This time I was unlucky but I knew I had some upstairs.

I put the package into my pocket and followed it with the old wrappings. That just left the cotton-wool and the diamonds. I folded the lot into a little bundle and then wrapped that into my handkerchief and tied a knot in it. I went back into the main room and put the little bundle into one of my shoes, slipped off my jacket and trousers and crawled back into bed with Carole.

She turned towards me and her fingers began to do what they had been doing earlier.

'Haven't you had enough?' I asked her.

She didn't answer. Christ, I thought, she's doing it in her sleep. So we did it in her sleep and in some ways it was better than it normally was because I didn't have to think too much about what I was doing.

That was just as well because most of my mind was on the meeting I had in a few hours time with the big man.

One way or another it looked like being an interesting day. Maybe my thirty-sixth year was getting off to a more promising start than any of its predecessors after all.

CHAPTER TWO

It was still dark when I slipped up the stairs and into my room. I dug around for a few minutes until I turned up a roll of Sellotape. Then I made a neat little parcel out of the tin box containing the paperback and took it down to the garage. I dropped the parcel down beside the seat where the big man had left it, then I selected a suitable hiding-place for the little wad of cotton-wool, complete with its contents.

I was doing things without any clear, conscious thought. Only one thing was certain in my mind; fate had dropped this little bundle in my lap and I wasn't about to hand it back.

I guessed that the little job the big man had for me was a simple delivery. He planned to get me to deliver the package to someone and pay me a few pounds for my trouble. Not too much so that I would get suspicious, but not so little that I would refuse. Forty, maybe fifty pounds. To do what? To deliver diamonds worth fifty thousand—more, for all I knew.

Anyway, when I saw him at the library he would collect his little packet, from where he presumably had accidently dropped it, offer me the deal and I'd take it. But not before I got him to sign his name, any name, across the wrapper. That way, when I made the delivery, I was in the clear. Whoever I delivered the phoney package to would blame the big man and the big man would blame him. No-one would suspect me because I would be clean. Clever? I thought so. Unfortunately, like a lot of things I've done in the past, I didn't think clearly enough, or far enough ahead. Not far enough at all.

Back in the house I went up to my room and made some coffee and thought about breakfast but there was a churning in my stomach that made food seem unappetising, particularly the odds and ends of stale bread and the few tins of stuff I had around. I was sitting there, drinking coffee and trying to control my stomach, when I heard the street door open and someone start up the stairs. In that instant I remembered the two coppers from the night before. How in God's name I'd managed to forget about them I don't know. Whatever it was they had wanted they were bound to come back. Like dogs with a stick to chase, they never give up.

Then my brain began to function normally and I realised only one person was coming up the stairs and the footsteps were not heavy. They stopped on the landing below and I heard a tapping on Carole's door. I eased open my door, slid onto the landing and looked down. It was a woman but from that angle I couldn't make out anything about her. I stepped back from the edge of the landing and as I did so she turned away from the door and started up the stairs towards me. I recognised her then, it was B. J. Williams. I'd met her a few times before, both at the theatre when I'd been backstage to collect Carole after the booze had got to her legs, and at the studios of the local radio station where B.J. worked. She was a producer—arts, I think.

The reason I'd been to the studios was because they ran a weekly jazz programme and the former presenter had regularly borrowed records from my collection. Every time I'd been to see him he'd been holding hands with B.J. and generally simpering at her like an adolescent, which, in some ways, was precisely what he was. Not that B. J. Williams wasn't worth an occasional simper—if you happen to like statuesque brunettes with legs all the way up and a figure that makes you want to take up sculpture. She wore her hair cropped fairly short and close to her head and in certain lights she looked like Cyd Charisse. Like I said, well worth the occasional simper.

Anyway, it turned out he had been telling his wife that the reason he was frequently kept late at the studio was that he was in conference with B. J. Williams. I suppose she must have thought that with a name like that, B.J. was a pipe-smoking, tweed-jacketed, former Welsh International prop forward—until the night she called at the studio herself. After that they had to get a new presenter for the jazz programme and my services hadn't been required any more.

'Hello, Johnny,' B.J. said as she reached my landing.

'B.J. Long time.'

'Yes. How are you?'

'Well enough. You?'

'Same.'

I replayed the opening remarks in my head. We seemed to be fencing and I wasn't sure why. 'Carole not up yet?' I asked.

'Seems not.'

'Must have had a hard night,' I said, trying not to sound as if that was my fault.

'Possibly. If you see her will you tell her I called and I'd like to talk to her.'

'Sure.'

'You will be seeing her?'

'I expect so. When I get back.'

'You're going out?'

'Yes.'

'Now?'

'Yes.'

'We can go together,' she said.

'I'll get my coat.' I went back into the room and picked up my jacket. When I turned round she had followed me into the room and was looking around with mildly curious eyes.

'You live alone,' she said.

It didn't sound like a question so I didn't answer it. Instead I said, 'Can I get you a cup of coffee?'

'Not unless you're having one.'

'I'm not.'

'Then we'd better go, if you have to be off.'

I looked at my watch. 'I'm not in too much of a hurry,' I said, thinking that if she had fancied the weed who had presented the jazz programme she wouldn't object too strongly to a tussle with me.

She looked at me, unblinkingly, for a moment. 'Another time,' she said, ambiguously.

We went down the stairs and into the street. I turned to go towards the garage and she followed me. After I had backed the car out she climbed in and I got out again to close the garage doors. When I got back in I glanced at her. She seemed a bit tense.

'Where?' I asked her.

'Where what?'

'Where do you want to go?'

'Oh. The studio will be fine. If you're going that way.'

'Okay.' I drove out and cut through a couple of back streets that bisected huge, open spaces which had once been crammed with back-to-backs with no lavatories. They'd demolished the tiny houses and moved the occupants to massive, amorphous estates on the north and east sides of the city, where they had not only indoor lavatories but central heating and garages and split-level cookers and where old ladies were afraid to go out of their own front doors after dark for fear of being mugged or worse. It's called progress and it's what we pay rates and taxes for. Still, who am I to complain? I don't pay all that much tax anyway.

I drove out into Ferensway and turned right, passing the point where I'd dropped the big man the night before. I tangled with the early morning traffic as we thundered into the one-way system and caused a couple of mild cases of apoplexy by stopping on a double yellow line to let B.J. out.

She went round to the pavement on my side of the car and leaned down to put her head in the window. An old man stopped in his tracks just behind her and stared at her raised rump with an expression that combined senile lust with fond memory.

'Call in and see me some time,' she said.

'You sound like Mae West.'

'I could teach her a thing or two.'

'Could you now?'

She didn't answer but straightened up and walked off, her long legs covering the ground easily. I watched her go and then glanced at the old fellow who was leaning against the wall of the post office looking as if he might have a heart attack at any moment and obviously not caring if he did.

I grinned at him and raised two fingers at the horn-blowing car driver behind me who had things on his mind that even the sight of B.J. Williams' bottom couldn't obliterate.

I drove on through the traffic and eventually made it to the library, parked on a meter, switched off the ignition and thought about B.J. Then I thought about the big man and his package and a nasty thought crossed my mind. I leaned over and glanced down beside the seat where B.J. had sat. The package was still there. I grinned at my distrust of her. After all, she'd come to the house to see Carole, not me and, as far as I knew, the only people who knew I'd met the man with the tattooed fingers were a few dozen hairy students from the Haworth Arms and members of the band. I glanced at my watch. It was time to be going. I locked the car carefully, put a couple of coins in the parking meter and went to the library.

An hour later I was still there and there was no sign of the big man. I went back to the car and sat in it and stared unseeingly out of the window. For the first time since I had found the diamonds realism dispelled the cloud of euphoria. Being careless enough to drop several thousand pounds worth of gems in the car of a moderately untrustworthy individual like me was one thing. Failing to turn up to get them back was a very different matter. I began to consider the possibilities. They were endless but fairly high on the list was the thought that the big man hadn't been careless. Maybe he'd dropped the package deliberately. I let my mind follow that particular line of reasoning. It made a lot of sense. He had the stones, why didn't matter—I never considered for a moment that he had them legitimately—and for some reason or other he wanted them out of the way but where he could get at them when he wanted to. When it was safe to do so.

I felt my stomach curl again. Diamonds, especially that many, might be a girl's best friend, but men killed for them. And others died.

I started the engine and listened to the starter screech and then I drove carefully and with a dry mouth until I was back in Park Street. I parked well short of the house and went the rest of the way on foot looking for lurking heavyweights with machine-guns in every doorway. I reached the house without being shot at and went up the stairs to my room. It didn't take me very long to pack away a few odds and ends of clothing and, as my personal possessions didn't amount to much, I was ready to go within five minutes. I eyed my record and casette playing equipment and my music collection regretfully and then decided that if I left them the landlord would probably sell them to pay the rent I owed. I piled them all onto the bed and went down the stairs to Carole's room.

She opened the door after several bangs that were louder than I liked. I was becoming extremely nervous.

'Christ, Johnny, do you know what time it is?'

'Noon,' I said.

'What day is it?'

'Wednesday.'

'What do you want?'

'I have to go out of town for a few days. I've a job in the Midlands.'

'When did that come up?'

'This morning. Look, I want to leave some of my stuff with you for safety. Okay?'

'Sure, bring it in.'

I spent five more valuable minutes ferrying my bits and pieces down to her room and then I brought down my battered suitcase. The one with the soft top with the tear in it and a label for the George Cinq Hotel in Paris, both of which were there when I'd picked it up in a junk shop.

'I'm off then.'

'Be good.'

'I expect I will. Oh, B.J. Williams called this morning. She wants to see you.'

Carole's face wrinkled in a frown but then the effort of so much thinking at that time of day was too much for her and she shrugged her shoulders, 'Okay, I'll call her.'

'I'll be seeing you,' I said and hesitated. I felt I ought to kiss her goodbye but I've never been able to work out precisely what our relationship amounted to.

'Yes,' she said, smiling unsteadily. 'Don't stay away too long, Johnny.'

'I won't,' I said and went down the stairs and along the street to the car. I threw the case in the back seat and climbed in. Then I slipped the big man's package in my pocket and before I had time to start the engine a police car drove up to the house. I stayed where I was, leaning forward with my hand on the ignition key and waited. One of the occupants, a uniformed constable, stayed in the car while the other, in plain-clothes, climbed out and went into the house.

I waited.

A couple of minutes later he reappeared and

34

got back into the car. It started up and rolled forward and passed me. I started to breathe again and turned the key. The starter made a noise that sounded like a million milk bottles being dropped from the top of a four-storey building and then stopped. In the silence that followed I heard the high-pitched whine of a car being driven in reverse. It was the law.

The one who had gone into the house climbed out and looked at the car, studiously avoiding my eyes until he had inspected every part of it for rust and every tyre for wear. Eventually he leaned down and looked in my window.

'Having trouble, sir?'

'Starter's packed up.'

'That's what it was, was it? Thought something sounded bad.' There was a silence while we both thought our own private thoughts. Then he cleared his throat noisily. 'Your car is it, sir?'

'Yes.'

'You'll have the registration particulars then. MOT and things like that?'

'Yes.'

'Maybe you'd like to show them to me.'

'They're at home.'

'And where's that?'

I thought desperately for a likely sounding address, not knowing why I had to lie but sensing that if I didn't I would be in trouble, and simultaneously knowing that I would only

35

make matters worse for myself later.

'I've just come into town,' I said, eventually. 'I'm looking for a room to rent.'

'Where have you come from?' he asked but just then his partner called out to him and he left me and went across to talk to him. I watched them out of the corner of my eye. Partner was writing something on a piece of paper fastened to a clip-board. I had a sinking feeling I knew what it was. After a few more moments, moments that seemed to drag on and on, the first copper came back and this time his mate got out of the car too and stood where I would have to drive over him if I wanted to get away.

The first one's head came back into my window. 'You didn't tell me your name,' he said.

I noticed he'd dropped the 'sir' bit. I grinned weakly. 'You didn't ask.'

'I'm asking now.'

I didn't need it spelling out for me. His partner had been checking my car's registration particulars. 'Baxter, John.'

'Address?'

I pointed at the house. 'There.'

He grunted and opened my door for me. 'Let's go,' he said, just to prove he watched the American cops and robbers' series on the box like everyone else.

'Why?' I asked, reasonably.

He showed me his teeth in what might have

been a smile in the days before he'd lost his sense of humour. 'Someone wants to talk to you.'

'Who?'

He sighed theatrically. 'Look, you're a big boy now.' He was at least ten years younger than I was but I let it pass. My involvement with the law was infrequent but it was enough to know that I could demand my rights for all they were worth and all that would happen would be a delay. A delay during which the law got itself into a frame of mind that wouldn't be in my best interests. I matched his sigh, climbed out and put the key into the door lock.

'What's in the case?' he asked.

'Socks and other unmentionables.'

'Open it up.'

I shrugged my shoulders and did as I was told. He poked around and then nodded. 'Okay.'

We all climbed into the police car and wound our way in silence across the city centre to police headquarters that stretched along one side of Queens Gardens. When we got there the talking one disappeared, leaving me in the entrance with his mate strategically placed between me and the door in case I tried to leave in a hurry.

Eventually, a weary-looking, uniformed sergeant appeared and jerked a thumb at me. I followed him along a corridor and he opened a door and I went in.

There are some people you like on sight and some you don't, some you trust and some you don't. The large, bearded bear-like man at the other side of the desk looked like one I would both like and trust at any time other than when I had someone else's, possibly stolen, diamonds hidden away.

'Sit down,' the bear said.

I sat down and looked at him.

He looked back at me like a kindly uncle and then shook his head sadly as if I'd let him down by stealing an apple from the vicar's tree. 'Naughty,' he said.

'What have I done?'

'You know that as well as I do.'

'Look, your lads got straight answers to all their questions.'

'Except the one about where you lived.'

'No law against that,' I said.

He pursed his lips and gave that as much consideration as if I'd been the Lord Chief Justice.

'Maybe not,' he said eventually. 'What company have you been keeping lately, Johnny?'

Now there are some things I can stand and some I can't and the casual assumption from certain coppers that they have a God-given right to call you by your first name whilst you have to grovel around and call them 'mister' or even 'sir' is one that gets right up my nose.

'I haven't anything to tell you,' I told him, shortly.

'Oh dear. Upset you have I? Well now, what can it be that I said.' He scowled in mock concentration. Then he beamed widely and showed me a couple of gold fillings. 'You didn't like me calling you Johnny did you, Johnny?' He waited and when I didn't say anything he leaned forward and folded his arms on the desk top. 'Right, Mr. Baxter, let's get down to business shall we?' There was no emphasis on the name, he seemed to be playing it straight so I had no choice but to play along. At least until I found out what it was he was after.

I nodded my head peaceably and waited.

'Do you know a man named Claude Jenks?'

That isn't the kind of name you forget once you've heard it so I didn't even need to think about it. 'No.'

'Really?'

'Really.'

'Mm.' He stared at me for a moment or two and then shrugged his heavy shoulders and levered himself up out of his chair. 'Come along,' he said. 'Let's go for a ride.' Erect, he seemed to fill the room. He patted the pockets of his hairy jacket, a piece of tailoring that looked as if it could have served as a winter comforter for a not very small elephant and glanced around the room. He scooped up a notebook and a few sheets of paper plus a fistful

39

of pencils and dropped them into the pockets, making the coat bulge even more than it did to start with. Then he shambled to the door and I followed him out and along the corridor into the street. His car, a surprisingly sedate and ancient Rover, was parked on a meter just by the main entrance. The penalty flag on the meter was showing but there was no sign of a ticket on the windscreen. The traffic warden hasn't been made who would risk booking a man like that. He clambered into the Rover, unlocked the passenger door for me and then started up and drove around the police building joining a queue of traffic trying to get into the city centre.

'You've been lucky,' he remarked, conversationally.

'Lucky?'

'You've never been in our hands.'

I felt my earlier irritation creeping back. 'The same can be said for a few million others. Are they lucky too?'

He gave that the same careful consideration he'd given some of my other remarks. 'No,' he said after a few moments. 'But then, they, or at least the majority of them, are leading normal lives.'

'And I'm not?'

'Are you?'

I leaned back in the seat and grinned widely. The big man was fishing. I didn't have a record

40

and at the very most my name might appear as a known associate of a few minor villains such as my friends of ten years before. Nothing there likely to be of interest to the big policeman. I relaxed. I knew there wasn't anything for him to get hold of, not until the matter of the diamonds anyway, and he couldn't possibly know about them.

'The life I lead,' I told him, 'is so normal the only surprising thing about it is that I don't die of boredom.'

'Is that so?'

'Yes, it is,' I said firmly.

We nudged along through the traffic for a while in silence.

'Maybe you *are* just a victim,' he said, eventually.

I looked at him, surprised at his choice of words. 'Victim?'

'Victim of circumstances,' he said, comfortably.

I didn't say anything. I was still certain he was fishing but until I knew what he wanted I would have to play things carefully. There was a lot more to the big man than I had thought. I wasn't sure what his attitude conveyed, but if he wanted me to feel uneasy he was succeeding.

I decided it was time to shift ground so I made it personal. 'I didn't think coppers wore beards,' I said.

'Optional,' he said, equably. It seemed he

wanted to be friends, after all he could have told me to mind my own business.

'I've not seen you around the town,' I remarked, implying he wasn't easy to miss, bulky, bearded and voluminously jacketed as he was. To say nothing of the gold fillings in his teeth.

'As a law-abiding citizen you wouldn't come across me.'

'That's been admitted into evidence then, has it?'

'What?'

'That I'm law-abiding.'

'For now.'

'I don't suppose you're going to tell me what all this is about are you?'

He turned and grinned at me, the gold fillings gleaming out of the bush around his face. 'What do you think?' he said, still amiable.

Neither of us spoke again for the ten or fifteen minutes it took him to negotiate the city centre and reach our destination.

It was the first time I'd been inside a mortuary. It isn't an experience I'm likely to want to repeat in a hurry.

I kept my eyes carefully to my front so that I only saw what I wanted to see and even then I wasn't one hundred percent successful.

The big bearlike policeman stopped beside a trolley that carried something covered in a sheet. Standing by the trolley was a tall, bony individual who looked as if he should have booked a permanent place there years before. He watched me with watery, wistful eyes which held a faint gleam that seemed to be trying to tell me something. Something like, one day I might end up there under one of *his* sheets.

Big bear nodded at bony who turned back the corner of the sheet with a practised flick of the wrist.

I made myself look down and a split-second before my eyes saw the face I knew who it was going to be.

'Know him?' the bear asked.

There didn't seem much point in lying. He hadn't brought me there for the fun of it. Somehow, and so far I hadn't a clue how he'd managed it, he had connected me with the man with the tattooed fingers.

'Yes,' I said.

'You said you didn't.'

I looked at him. Big brown eyes were watching me, not missing anything from the flicker I could feel along my eyelids to the sweat droplets that were starting up on my forehead. 'Claude Jenks?' I asked. He nodded slowly. 'He didn't tell me his name,' I added.

Bear nodded again. 'But you've seen him before?'

'Yes.'

'When?'

'Last night.'

There was a long silence. 'What time and where did you see him last?' he said eventually.

I told him. Then I added, inconsequentially, 'He was alive when I left him.'

He nodded as if agreeing with me. Then, just to show he wasn't necessarily doing anything of the sort, he said. 'If you left him in Ferensway then I expect he was. That isn't where we found him.'

'Where did you find him?'

'Tell me where you met him, how and why,' he said, ignoring my question.

I told him about the big man's telephone call and I told him about the scene in the pub. After all, if I didn't, there were enough people there who wouldn't have much difficulty in remembering him. And me. Needless to say I didn't tell him about the package the big man had left in my car.

As I told the story I was aware that the fake package I'd made up was still in my pocket. That would be a joke, if they searched me. A carefully wrapped-up parcel containing a tin box with a paperback novel in it. Huge joke. Except that the dead man's fingerprints might very well be all over the tin box unless I'd smudged them sufficiently.

When I'd finished, big bear nodded wisely as if all I had done was confirm something he already knew.

'That's everything is it?' he asked.

44

'Yes.'

'And you'd never met Jenks before last night?'

'No.'

'Mm. I don't suppose you'd forget anyone like this anyway. Would you?'

The last two words were accompanied by a nod to bony who flicked his wrist again and uncovered the big man's entire body.

I stared at it. The tattooing didn't stop at his fingers. It ran all the way up his arms and across his shoulders and then down his chest and belly. His thighs were covered in black, blue, green and red loops and scrolls, faces and birds and animals. A regular picture gallery.

I looked up at the bear. 'No, I wouldn't forget anyone like that,' I said.

'That's what I thought,' he said, turning and walking away.

I followed him after trying a courteous nod to bony who gave me a brief, contemptuous glance that told me he would have a place for me anytime I cared to die.

Big bear waited at the door and we walked out in silence. It was drizzling outside and it was cold but even so it was a pleasure to be in the open after the dead, dank air of the mortuary.

'You weren't planning on leaving town, were you?' he asked.

I guessed he knew about the suitcase in my car. 'No,' I said. 'Not now.'

45

'Good.' He started to walk towards his car.

'Is that it?' I called after him.

He stopped and turned round, regarding me with frank and unblinking brown eyes. 'Unless your memory takes a turn for the better,' he said.

He waited and we looked at one another. Then he shrugged, climbed into his car and drove off into the drizzle.

I watched until he was out of sight and then I looked at the big doors we had come through and thought about the big man. Claude Jenks. It didn't seem a very likely name for a man like that.

On reflection, I realised I didn't know the name of the big policeman. Apparently he hadn't thought it necessary to tell me such intimate details about himself, but he had made it clear he wanted me where he could reach me. That meant my hastily reached decision to get out of town had to be abandoned. Just how the big man planned to implement his relatively polite suggestion that I stay around was something I didn't know, but it wasn't something I was prepared to risk finding out. Not while I had a parcel of someone else's diamonds.

Unwilling though I was, there wasn't any doubt that I would be wise to stay where I was. If I ran for it I would have the police to contend with and hiding out isn't as easy as it might appear to be. Getting out of the country for someone like me, a man with no connections to speak of, was next to impossible.

I needed a clear field to allow me to unload the diamonds with a minimum of risk and a maximum of profit and once again I didn't have connections. I would need time to find a big-time fence who could handle the stones and doing that with policemen breathing down my neck didn't seem a very good idea.

It looked as if I would be better off staying where I was until the police lost interest in me, but that meant I needed to know more about Jenks. I had a vested interest in knowing who he was, where he came from, who his friends were, and, most important of all, who his enemies were. As long as I had his diamonds, there was a good chance that his enemies would make themselves my enemies too.

I tried to think where I could start and the only hope seemed to be the tattoos. It wasn't much, but while I might not have connections that would help me get out of the country or fence a parcel of gemstones, I did have connections that might help me there.

CHAPTER THREE

Almost directly across the road from the mortuary is the Humberside Theatre which, from the outside, looks just about as inviting. As the time of day, added to recent events, seemed to indicate refreshment of some kind, I went in. I leaned on the bar along with the only other early drinker, a morose, scrawny individual whose Adam's apple bobbed frequently as he swallowed insipid-looking lager. I counted my loose change. I couldn't really afford it but I bought myself a scotch and conducted a brief, silent, wake for the recently departed Claude Jenks.

I tried to add up what I knew and what was likely to happen next. I've never been very good at sums and this time proved to be no exception. For a start the tattooed man was a mixture of contradictions. Someone with a pocketful of diamonds doesn't usually go around attracting attention to himself and there was little doubt that that was precisely what Jenks had been doing at the pub. The language and the manners were an act, I was sure of that, but why? Add to that the fact that people carrying packets of gemstones worth thousands of pounds don't accidentally drop them in a car belonging to someone they've never met before. He'd done that deliberately too.

Then there was the policeman who'd just left me to my own devices. He didn't add up either. He had a dead body, one he'd been able to identify, which meant Jenks was carrying identification of some kind, although whether or not Jenks was his real name was another matter. Jenks must have had my name and address or at least my telephone number on him, which was logical, but what wasn't logical was that the big policeman hadn't leaned on me.

I looked at a pile of sausage rolls under a clear plastic dome but all they did was remind me of the tattooed man's fingers. I counted my change again, just to make sure and regretfully swallowed the last of my drink and went out.

The drizzle had eased a little but there was still enough to gradually seep through my trousers. My leather jacket was becoming a bit soggy but so far hadn't begun to leak, although it was probably only a matter of time. I trudged across the centre of the city and eventually wound my way to a scrap yard off Green Lane. I spent a fingernail-breaking half hour scrambling over a pile of cars waiting to be re-cycled, or whatever the current phrase is for smashing them into little pieces, and eventually managed to find a Cortina the same age as mine. I borrowed a pair of spanners and took out the starter.

The scrap-yard owner listened to my tale of

woe without expression, but as I'd bought stuff from him before and always paid up in the end he let me take the starter away without paying for it. I left him scratching the ears of a maniacal-looking Alsatian and mentally put him to the top of the list of my creditors. I didn't fancy letting him take the price of the starter out of my backside with the aid of the dog.

Back in Park Street nobody had bothered to take the wheels off the Cortina in my absence and I spent the rest of the afternoon replacing my duff starter. By five o'clock I had wheels again.

I humped my suitcase back into the house and up to the top floor. There was no sound from Carole's room, but I didn't knock on the door. I'd decided it was time to find Big Eric.

I drove west, parked the car in the car-park at the back of the supermarket on the Priory Road roundabout and walked the short distance to the house in North Road where my Uncle Sid and Aunt Doris lived. Sid and Doris Perkins are not really related to me but I've known them since I was about four years old and that's the way I've always referred to them. Doris was in and busy baking, that was no surprise, she always was. In fact, I can't ever remember seeing her in another room, always the kitchen.

She let me in with a warm, delighted smile that split a round, shining face which looked as if somebody had just finished painting it bright red. She's about five feet tall and built like one of the farmhouse loaves she bakes. She wears wire-rimmed glasses that look as if they were bought in Woolworths in the days before Do-It-Yourself optical prescribing was banned. Her hair looked the way it always does, like an exploding Brillo pad.

'When did you last eat?' she asked me as I sat down at the cluttered kitchen table.

'Breakfast,' I lied.

'Which day?' she asked, to prove she didn't believe me without actually saying so.

I grinned at her. 'Three weeks last Monday.'

She sniffed loudly and tried to frown but she didn't have the face for it. Twenty minutes later I had eaten myself to a standstill and was on my third mug of tea.

'Big Eric in town?' I asked eventually, leaning back in the hard chair and trying to remember the last time I'd eaten so well. Probably not since my last visit there.

'Due back tonight or tomorrow,' she said. 'Fair week, next week.'

I nodded, I'd forgotten it was almost that time of year. The fair comes to Hull every October, second week in the month, never misses. It's been coming since the Middle Ages and if you're thinking of a couple of roundabouts and a Bingo stall, think again. Along with Nottingham's annual Goose Fair it's the biggest in Europe and worth a visit or even two. At least two for

51

anyone wanting to try everything. Big Eric worked for a small family-owned circus that still managed to keep going and who were usually to be found in a corner of the fairground.

I'd better explain about Big Eric. Real name, Sid Perkins, four feet ten and a half inches tall in the black plimsolls he never seemed to take off. To me, he's always looked the same, bright eyed and bald-headed although I'd known him fifteen years before I'd realised he was bald. He took his cap off about as often as he took off his plimsolls. I haven't a clue how old he was, maybe sixty-five or so, and permanently smiling, like his wife. A different smile though, because he didn't have any teeth of his own and refused to wear the perfectly good false set he carried, neatly wrapped in a blue-spotted handkerchief, in his coat pocket.

He'd been born into a travelling-show family and never knew any other life. Fairs, circuses, music-halls, always one or the other and almost always backstage. It was in a brief spell in the music-hall that he went on-stage for the first and only time in his life. On the bill was a double-act, a pair of knock-about comics billed as Mighty Joe and Big Eric. Mighty Joe was a midget and Big Eric was a dwarf, a difference not many people appreciate. One night the dwarf broke his arm and as a last-minute substitute Sid Perkins went on in his place. Even at his height he was too big but he was the nearest they could get at short notice, if you'll pardon the pun. He partnered the midget for six weeks until the dwarf came back and never again went on-stage. But ever after he was known as Big Eric to everyone, except his wife. I don't know whether he objected or not, he didn't seem to, but then conversation with Big Eric wasn't easy. Although he was bright and intelligent and could hear a pound note being folded at fifty paces, he was dumb. He was born that way and had never spoken a word in his life. Pity, he probably had more than a few tales to tell.

'I want a word with him,' I told Doris.

'Important?' She wasn't being idly inquisitive, she merely wanted to place my request on the list in order of priority. Big Eric came home no more than five or six times a year and there were usually a hundred and one things that needed his attention.

I thought about her question for a moment. There didn't seem a lot of point in pretending it wasn't important, the way things were anything could happen, and very probably would, without a lot of warning.

'Yes,' I said. 'Could be.'

She looked at me shrewdly. 'Are you in trouble again?'

I grinned at her. 'Me? In trouble, come on now.'

Her smile dimmed fractionally. 'It's been

53

known,' she said quietly.

I nodded, serious, after all there was no point in kidding her, of all people. 'Just a problem that can be handled, but I need some information and Big Eric might be the one to help me.'

'I'll tell him. Are you still in that same place?'

I thought back to my last visit, over six months before. 'No, I've moved.' I wrote down the address and the telephone number. She took it and sniffed when she saw the address. I knew what that meant, she hadn't thought much of my last place of residence and this one was another step downwards.

'Call me if he comes in,' I said. 'If someone else answers the 'phone just leave your name, I'll know what it's about.'

She folded the piece of paper and tucked it away in her apron pocket. 'Just be careful,' she said.

'I will.'

We sat and talked for a while, or rather I sat and Doris hurtled around the kitchen baking more and more cakes and loaves. They had three sons, all of them my age group but, unlike me, none of them had ever married. Oddly enough they were all big men, not one under six feet and with appetites like Shire horses. I expect that was why they hadn't married. Finding a woman with the culinary capabilities of their mother would have been a fairly hopeless task for any one of them. For all three it was impossible, they don't make 'em like Doris Perkins any more.

'Have you seen Sandra or Susie recently?' she asked, cutting into my daydreaming.

'No, not for a while.' I thought about it. 'Not since I was here last,' I added. 'We've talked once or twice on the telephone though.'

'When?'

'Last time? The other day.'

'Had she anything to tell you?'

I started to answer, then realised that Doris was digging. That was unusual, she wasn't the nosey type.

'Should she have?' I asked. With her high colour she couldn't turn any redder than she was normally but her clattering about became even wilder than usual. 'Well?'

'I heard she was thinking of marrying again,' she said, eventually.

'Oh.' Not a very intelligent remark but it gave me a moment to think. I tested my reaction to Doris's information. There didn't seem to be any, except, possibly, a feeling of mild relief that the problem of raking together the maintenance money might soon be a thing of the past. That reminded me of the conversation I'd had with Sandra and it seemed as if it might be an explanation of her apparent indifference to how much I sent her. Maybe she was merely concerned that my payments were up to date by

55

the time I learned of any impending change in her marital state.

'Probably for the best all round,' Doris said.

'I expect you're right.'

'It's time you did the same.'

'What?'

'It's time you married again. It isn't right for a man to stay single.' I opened my mouth to comment that her own sons were not a very good advertisement for that particular philosophy, but she beat me to it. 'Don't tell me about my three. That's different, they know when they're onto a good thing. You're not living in comfort and getting three square meals a day, are you?'

I shook my head. 'No, I'm not.'

'And living in those awful rooms.'

I nodded.

'And the company you keep.'

I raised an eyebrow at her because that had to be pure guesswork. She didn't know anything about the company I kept but I couldn't argue with the accuracy of her assessment of my usual friends and acquaintances. It brought my mind back to Carole and the on-off relationship we seemed to have developed. I was mildly grateful that Doris didn't know about Carole. I guessed that would have precipitated an explosion which might have ruined the day's output from the cooker. As it was Doris was plainly feeling uneasy at the fact that she was intruding into my life. I didn't mind, I knew that she was doing it only because she thought I needed someone to tell me right from wrong. She might very well have been right about that.

I suppose she was also correct in saying that I needed some kind of permanent relationship and a reasonable place to live. The trouble was that after ten or eleven years living more or less alone I wasn't sure I wanted anyone around on a regular basis. I wouldn't go so far as to say that I liked the way I lived, after all I wasn't a masochist, but I had grown accustomed to it. The only things I felt I really needed were a change of environment and an improvement in my financial well-being. With luck both might be within my reach, very soon.

'I expect you're right about that as well,' I told Doris.

'But you're not going to do anything about it?'

'Maybe I will, and maybe sooner than you think.'

'Let's hope so,' she said, a shade primly but I could tell she was pleased, even if she wasn't sure she believed me.

I stood up and gave her a kiss. 'Thanks, love,' I told her. 'Message received and understood.' She dabbed me on the cheek with her hand and I wiped off a patch of flour she left behind.

I left, not wanting to be there when her family came in, they were all friendly, cheerful men, and when I was younger we had all been good friends, but just then I didn't feel like an evening's reminiscing.

Instead I climbed into the Cortina and rattled back into town. I wasn't in any particular hurry to get anywhere and I took my time. That was why I noticed a car that appeared to be following me. It was an Escort estate, dark blue and innocuous, but I got a funny feeling about it. I made a few random turns that didn't make any kind of sense and the Escort stayed with me.

I began to get anxious.

I had a sudden vision of the anticipatory gleam in the eye of the mortuary attendant and headed smartly back onto a main, well-lit, road.

It was almost seven o'clock by then and I reckoned that I needed bright lights and people around me. I parked the car on double yellow lines just across the road from the local radio station's studios, safe in the knowledge that the parking meter attendants had crawled back into their holes for the night. I glanced up at the lighted windows of the studios and thought about taking up B.J. Williams' offer of that morning, but then thought better of it. I needed to find out who was following me, or lose him, first. I spotted the blue Escort trying to make itself invisible about fifty yards away, just around the corner in Paragon Street and I wandered off in the other direction, giving the driver ample time to lock up and follow me.

I went all the way around the block until I came up behind his car and memorised the registration number. Then I crossed the road and went into the ground floor bar of The Hull Cheese. Noise hit me like a solid wall. I can take most kinds of music but anything several hundred decibels above the pain threshold doesn't do a lot for me. I tried to think about something else, without much success, and elbowed my way towards the bar before I remembered I was too low on cash to run to even a glass of beer. I came to a halt and let myself be jostled and pushed until I was in a corner where I could see the door and anyone who came through it.

I didn't have long to wait before my shadow joined the crush. He was as much out of place as I was among that teenaged, extravagantly-dressed, loud-talking mob and I recognised him immediately. He looked just as morose as he had when I'd seen him, earlier that day, sipping lager, in the bar at the Humberside Theatre.

I worked my way a few more inches backwards and leaned against the wall trying to think what his presence on the scene proved, if anything. The deafening roar stopped fleetingly as the record on the juke-box changed, but the silence didn't last long. From somewhere or other someone had got hold of an old Ike and Tina Turner record and *Hold on Baby* was soon threatening to perforate my eardrums. I can stand a lot of Ike and Tina, particularly Tina, but there's a limit, especially when I can't get my hand on the volume control so, having identified my shadow, I decided to shuffle off into the night.

I'm not sure why, having identified him, I should feel any easier, but I did. I was back at the Cortina before my conscious caught up with my subconscious. He had to be a copper. He'd been in the bar at the theatre before I was, which meant that he was one of the big bear's men.

Identification of the gloomy-looking man who was trailing me, coupled with the near-certainty that he was a policeman seemed oddly reassuring.

I decided to go home and worry in my room, safe in the knowledge that my man in the blue Escort would very probably spend a cold night outside watching over me.

When I went up the stairs past Carole's door I heard music and glued my ear there for a moment, thought I heard heavy breathing and crept on up the next flight. If she was entertaining it wouldn't do to disturb her—or her companion. If I interrupted at a crucial moment he might feel his contract had been broken and who was I to come between an honest, working girl and her source of income?

I sat in my room and for the first time for some months the true squalor of the place was apparent to me. I expect it was reaction from the warmth, friendliness and cleanliness of Doris Perkins' little house. I wandered about and made a couple of stabs at tidying up but I soon tired of that. I made some coffee and sat down again. I felt the package I'd faked-up in my pocket, pulled it out and looked at it. There didn't seem to be much point in keeping it so I heaved it into the corner of the room that serves as a waste-paper basket. Then I stood up again and picked it up and brought a knife from the kitchen-alcove that was even tinier than the one in the room below and opened up the package. I opened the tin box intending to take out the paperback novel I'd borrowed from Carole. It wasn't there.

I felt my mouth go dry and the hairs on the back of my neck stand up. For a few tortured seconds I thought I was seeing the work of the supernatural. Carole's paperback novel had been replaced by a neat, thick wad of twenty-pound notes.

CHAPTER FOUR

There were three hundred twenty-pound notes in the little box. Six thousand pounds. I counted it twice to make sure. Then I made myself another cup of coffee, peered through the window to see if my protector was out there, saw that he was and stretched out on the bed to try to work out what had happened, and why.

The 'what' was fairly easy—it was the 'why' that caused most trouble.

Obviously Jenks had been using me as an unwitting post office. He never had any intention of offering me a job. He had dropped the package containing the diamonds in the car for someone else to collect and replace with the package containing the money.

But it hadn't worked out that way. I'd found the package, made the substitution and when the 'switcher' had arrived on the scene, he, or she, had made off with a paperback novel. Six thousand pounds for a paperback. Someone wasn't going to be very happy about that, not very happy at all.

I still couldn't see 'why' so I thought, instead, about 'who'. Without doubt B.J. Williams was top of the list. She was the only person to have been in the car since I had dropped the big man, or rather, I corrected myself, to give her the benefit of some doubt, the only person I *knew* had been in it. The car had been left, unattended, outside the library for over an hour, which could have been part of the plan. Breaking into a car is a lot easier than most people believe. I know, I've opened the occasional car door myself when times were hard.

So, that left me with an unanswered, 'why'. I couldn't see any logic in any of it and after half an hour or so I gave up and dozed off, still fully dressed and woke a few hours later thinking I was freezing to death.

I stood up, turned out the light and checked if my watcher in the blue Escort was still there. He wasn't. I felt an absurd sense of loss, followed rapidly by a sense of fear that I was exposed. Exposed to whoever had just paid out six thousand pounds for an evening's light reading.

I was tempted to run for it again and for several long minutes I argued with myself. Eventually I decided against it. Running, when I didn't know who was likely to chase after me, didn't seem a very good idea although I felt an almost overwhelming desire to go and chance it. I convinced myself that running in the dark with unknown pursuers was not a very bright plan and I also convinced myself it was an intelligent decision. It didn't prevent a nagging suspicion that all I had done was to uncover an unsuspected streak of masochism inside me.

I made sure the door was locked and for good measure propped a chair under the handle, the way they do in the movies, and spent the rest of the night trying to stay awake. Around six o'clock I made yet another cup of coffee, which emptied the jar, and sat in the little curtained-off alcove, with the light on, carefully re-packing the money. Not all of it, I kept out five of the twenties for working expenses. The rest, once re-packed in the tin and wrapped and sellotaped securely, I addressed to myself at Doris and Sid Perkins' address. I put the package in my pocket and folded the hundred pounds I needed into a small wad which I put in the heel of my shoe, something that probably came from the same movie as the chair under the door handle and was probably just as much a waste of time.

I hung around the room until I reckoned one or more of the little shops along Spring Bank would be open and then I went out, on foot, warily watching every doorway and parked car.

I bought a newspaper at the first newsagent I came to and walked on towards the nearest post-box. Under cover of the newspaper I fished the package out from my pocket and dropped it in the box. No stamp; if you want to be sure the Post Office does its duty, leave off the stamp. They'll take more care to deliver that than any registered letter.

Then I tramped back to the garage and drove to the scrapyard where I'd got the starter. I knew the owner always carried a large wad of notes, enough to choke his Alsatian with if the need ever arose.

I had to wait outside for him to arrive and when he did he looked faintly amused as I did a hasty check of the area before I took the notes from my shoe.

I told him I wanted them changing into fives and ones. He sniffed and looked at the dog which was eyeing my left leg longingly. 'Do you reckon they're real?' he asked the Alsatian.

I answered for the dog. 'Definitely.'

'Stolen then?'

The dog didn't answer that one either. 'Not that you'd notice,' I volunteered.

'Marked?'

I hesitated and then decided there was nothing to be gained by lying about that one. I didn't have many friends and while the scrap-dealer wasn't exactly a friend he wasn't an enemy either. 'Doubt it, but if they are it isn't by the police.'

He thought about that for a while, then he asked the dog, 'Fifty percent sound right to you?'

I don't know what the dog thought about it, but I know what I did. 'Balls,' I said.

He looked at me for the first time and grinned. 'Okay,' he said. 'Just trying you out for honesty. If it really was slush or marked you'd be only too glad to get shot of it to argue.'

'Tell you what I'll do,' he said. He fumbled in his pocket and brought out the dog-choking roll. He peeled off a few notes. 'There's seventy-five. If nobody scratches around during the next few days I'll top it up to ninety. The tenner's for the starter.'

I took the money. My only reason for

65

changing it was that I didn't want to be seen spending twenties. Not until I knew whose they were.

I left him scratching his dog's ears and went in search of food. I settled for a bacon sandwich in a cafe near the river and washed it down with a mug of tea that seemed to have been pumped straight from the turgid water that flowed beyond the adjacent concrete wharf.

It was fairly high on my list of action to talk to B.J. Williams but I didn't fancy making a too direct approach. I felt that a chance encounter might be best and so instead of going to the radio station's studios I went over to the theatre where I had picked up my tail of the previous day.

There wasn't much sign of activity but I could hear someone singing *Indian Love Call* in a cracked soprano. I pushed open the doors into the auditorium and traced the voice to a cleaner wandering along the rows of seats making an ineffectual stab at sweeping up last night's cigarette ends.

'Anyone else about?' I asked her.

She looked up at me and stopped serenading the Indians. 'Only me,' she said.

'What time does the gang get here?'

She didn't ask me who the gang was, which was just as well. 'Ten, half-past, there'll be somebody here by then. Lazy buggers.' She propped a hip against a chair and looked as if she was prepared to spend the intervening hour or two regaling me with her personal philosophy so I said my thanks and beat a hasty retreat.

In the foyer I glanced at the posters and photographs advertising coming attractions and had reached the door before what my eyes had just seen reached the part of my skull my brains hide in.

I let the door swing closed and went back to one of the photographs. The man was made-up and looked a little bit different but there wasn't much doubt about it. The morose-looking man who had trailed me, from the theatre all round the town and back home again, hadn't been a copper after all. He was an actor. According to the writing on the photograph his name was Joe Cornwell. I'd never heard of him.

Just about then I would have yelled, help, if I'd thought anyone would've answered. It was all getting too much for me.

I went out of the theatre, planning to climb into the Cortina and look for a hole to hide in.

CHAPTER FIVE

I didn't get very far. In fact I didn't get any further than my car. Someone was waiting by the kerb and even with high boots and a long coat I could detect the lines of the body that had driven the local radio station's jazz programme presenter out of his, admittedly, tiny mind.

'Hello B.J.,' I said, trying not to look at her with the expression of a man who thought she was responsible for switching the substitute diamond package.

'I thought it was your car, Johnny. Been to the theatre?'

Since she'd seen me come out of the front door it seemed as if we were in for another of those oddly stilted conversations.

'Yes,' I said, and waited to see where we went next.

'There wouldn't be anyone there at this time of day.'

The conversation was getting worse. 'Another lift?' I asked. Anything to get away from there.

She thought about the question with more care than it seemed to warrant.

'I was planning on seeing the producer of this week's play,' she said, after a while.

'There isn't anyone there at this time of day.'

She didn't seem to notice I was repeating her own words of a second or two before. 'Oh,' she said.

I screamed silently and then in desperation said, 'We could go somewhere and get laid.'

She looked at me directly for the first time and there was more in her eyes than she'd managed to put into words during every conversation we'd ever had together. 'Was that a serious suggestion?'

I grinned at her. 'If the answer's yes, it was serious; if the answer's no, then it wasn't. After all, I have my pride.'

'So have I,' she said remotely. Then she nodded her head. 'Okay, your place or mine?'

I tried not to look surprised and decided that if I wanted a hole to hide in I could do a lot worse. 'Yours,' I said. 'My cleaning lady hasn't been in since 1957.'

She waited, like a lady, until I opened the door for her, like a gentleman. It all seemed vaguely unreal. I glanced at my watch as I walked round to climb into my seat. Before nine o'clock on a cold and miserable October morning didn't seem a very likely time to be playing house with a glamorous and apparently highly-sexed young woman. But then, take things as you find them is my motto, especially where sex is concerned.

B.J. had a flat in a well-preserved house overlooking Pearson Park, an area that still retained a faded, genteel air that suited its late-Victorian appearance. The flat had two rooms plus a small kitchen and an even smaller shower room. They were high-ceilinged and well-decorated and furnished. They made the seedy rooms I'd spent most of my life in seem even worse than usual.

'Nice,' I said.

'Mm.'

'Been here long?'

'Nearly two years.'

'Oh.' Christ, I thought, these sparkling conversations will crucify me if they keep up.

She drifted into the kitchen and I heard the sound of a kettle being filled. I caught a glimpse of myself in a mirror. I looked like something cast out by the taggerine man. I wandered in the direction of the shower room and fingered various chromium-plated fittings.

'Plenty of hot water if you want one.' She had come up behind me, silently.

'I wouldn't mind,' I said. I was thinking that if we really were about to have a scramble in the sheets it wouldn't be a bad idea to scrape off some of the accumulated grime of the last couple of days and relatively sleepless nights. B.J. looked like the kind of woman who would prefer the touch of a stain-free human body. Always assuming she wasn't having some obscure joke with me.

She nodded and went out, closing the door behind her. I looked at the door, then shrugged and turned on the shower. She was right, it was hot. The room began to fill with steam and I swiftly slipped out of my clothes, stepped under the spray and pulled the shower-curtain across. I felt better when I turned off the shower and pulled back the curtain. Then I stopped feeling better. My clothes had gone.

I dried myself slowly, working out the

possible implications. When I had finished I had a few possibilities but, as far as I could see, investigating all of them necessitated walking out of the shower room with nothing between me and whoever or whatever waited outside but a towel. A very wet one at that.

I took a deep breath and opened the door. The main room was empty.

I listened. Faintly, I could hear music, it seemed to be coming from the bedroom. A voice too. Then a tinkling bell, like a telephone being replaced. I padded across the carpet towards the bedroom door, reflecting that to have walked barefoot across the floor of my room would have resulted in my feet being dirtier afterwards than they had been to start with, and very probably with passengers too.

I opened the door, prepared for the worse. B.J. was in bed, the sheet draped carefully across her hips but with a lot of one leg showing, together with everything from the hips up. She looked like a centrefold picture in a girlie magazine. I swallowed and looked round the room, looking for the photographers.

'Better?' she asked.

'What? Oh, yes. Much. Thanks.' There was a telephone by the bed. Maybe she *had* been talking to someone. There was a jug of what seemed to be coffee, a bottle of scotch and two glasses beside the bed. From some expensive-looking stereo equipment faint sounds of

Johnny Mathis were emerging. I had another look for the photographers. It was all too good to be true, like the set of a blue movie.

I spotted my clothes, at least some of them, on a chair. They were the only things in there that looked real. Grubby, but real.

'Are you going to stand there all morning?' she asked.

I looked at her and as I did she raised her arms above her head and stretched, thrusting her breasts forward at me. I swallowed again, this time I didn't bother about searching for hidden cameras. If they were there, then good luck to them.

I lasted longer than I expected I would and when we stopped I was as limp as if I'd been de-boned. I lay in a heap with B.J.'s long and powerful legs wrapped around my middle. I couldn't have moved if I'd wanted to. I didn't want to. I was happy but I wasn't sure about her. She had maintained a slightly detached air all the way through and I wondered why. I started to push myself free and she stopped me.

'Not yet,' she said.

I reached out an arm for the scotch and the two glasses and she eased her legs enough to let me pour out measures that would either kill or restore. They restored, and we were soon at it again.

This time she seemed to have her mind more on what we were doing and long before I was

72

finished she was bucking and heaving under me, a drone of relatively mild obscenities accompanying her movements.

I moved into a position where I could see her face.

'Well?' I asked.

'Well what?'

I shrugged. 'Be like that,' I said.

'Don't tell me you want congratulating.' There was an unpleasant tone in her voice.

'No, that isn't what I wanted. It's just that, well, our conversation doesn't exactly sparkle does it?'

'Is that what you came here for? Conversation.'

I began to feel irritable. 'Christ,' I said, struggling until I was sitting upright. 'Okay, let me out and I won't bother you again.'

She reached out and gripped my arm. 'I'm sorry, Johnny,' she said, suddenly contrite. 'I don't usually do this kind of thing at the drop of a few well-chosen words.'

'Or even ill-chosen ones,' I said.

She smiled, a real smile for the first time. I leaned over and kissed her and that was different too; a warm, yielding kiss. Then the telephone rang. Just once and then it stopped but I felt her tense and the tension didn't relax when the bell stopped. She pulled away from me, swung her long and beautiful legs off the bed, stood up and strode away, picking up her clothes as she went.

'I have to go and see that producer,' she said, over her shoulder. 'I'll be late.'

I scrambled off the bed, feeling righteously indignant and started to dress. Then I found my shirt and underpants had vanished. I opened my mouth to protest but her head came around the edge of the door.

'Some of your stuff was pretty foul,' she said. 'Try the cupboard over there. I think they should be your size.'

Her head disappeared again before I could object to her casual, sudden, and unjustifiable proprietorialness over my habits. I stamped across to the cupboard and she was right, there were a couple of shirts and a few other odds and ends, including underwear. I assumed they were the left-overs of lover-boy. Unwillingly I picked out a yellow, red and purple check shirt; I remembered he'd had rotten dress-sense, and even more reluctantly I pulled on a pair of his underpants. Odd really, I'd just spent a hot and hectic hour screwing his former girlfriend but I drew the line at putting on his underwear, even though they'd obviously been laundered since he last wore them.

By the time I was dressed, B.J. Williams was standing by the door jingling a key ring with a nervous agitation that did nothing to restore my fading sense of amiability towards her.

She opened the door and we went out in

silence. When we reached my car I stopped, but she strode on.

'Don't you want a lift?' I asked.

She paused and looked back. 'I suppose so,' she said.

'Christ, what's got into you? I thought it was men who were supposed to suffer from post-coital depression.'

'What?'

'Feeling miserable after fucking,' I snarled at her.

'There's no need to talk like that,' she snapped back.

I looked at her for a long moment and despite my anger I began to fancy her again. Then a nasty thought crossed my mind.

'This producer, you're seeing. His name wouldn't be Joe Cornwell, would it?'

She looked startled. 'No, he ... he's just an actor.' Her face had turned pink and she nodded quickly at the car. 'Alright, give me a lift into town.'

We did the first part of the journey in silence. Then I got tired of the strained atmosphere and fiddled with the cassette player and treated her, full volume, to *Inferno* by Louie Bellson's Big Band. She looked quite pale when I let her out at the theatre and I felt childishly pleased.

I watched her stride into the theatre and decided that I was sorry I hadn't made an impression on her. I thought back over the events in her bedroom and formed a couple of unpleasant conclusions. I reckoned I'd been taken for a ride—in a manner of speaking.

I drove away from the theatre, past the doors to the mortuary and into St. Stephen's Square. As soon as I could I bumped the Cortina up over a kerb and into a little corner where, with any amount of luck, the boys with the yellow bands on their caps wouldn't see it for the short time I expected it to be there. Then I walked swiftly back to the theatre.

There's usually a fairly good crowd in the bar of the Humberside Theatre on Thursday lunchtimes. In the room that opens off the bar— they pretentiously call it the gallery—they have a jam session. More often than not the music is predictable and dull but occasionally a spark is struck and the music lifts. Either way, dull or exciting, the main reason it's well-attended is that it's free. Not the booze or the food of course, just the music.

I pushed my way cautiously through the foyer keeping a careful eye out for either B.J. or Joe Cornwell. I didn't see either of them. I ordered a scotch and asked the young woman behind the bar if the producer was around.

'Haven't seen him yet, love.'

'If he comes in, point him out to me will you? I want a word.'

'Okay.' She rattled off down the bar dispensing beer and sausage rolls to the mob.

I turned away and went into the room where the band were ploughing into a stolid version of *Who's Sorry Now?* I decided I was, for one. A couple of the musicians were refugees from the band at the Haworth Arms the night I'd met Claude Jenks; the bass-player, still inaudible, and the man with the battered cornet. I hoped he wouldn't notice me.

After a few minutes they thumped to a stop with a predictable four-bar drum break from a weed with Shemp glasses and a Ho Chi-Minh beard. I went back to the bar and ordered another drink while they decided what they were going to play next. A few of the band were replaced by musicians who'd come in for a blow. One was a trumpet player and the cornettist dropped out and began to make his way to the bar. I tried to hide behind my glass, but he'd seen me.

He ordered a pint of beer and leaned towards me. 'Going to make a nuisance of yourself here?' he asked.

'Who, me?'

He treated me to what was supposed to be a glare from his slightly thyroid eyes but his heart wasn't in it. 'I suppose it was the other fellow's fault,' he acknowledged.

The girl behind the bar tapped me on the shoulder. 'That's him,' she said.

I turned round and saw a character in a corduroy jacket, pink shirt and sandals. I thought that kind of theatrical mannerism had gone out about the time Vanessa Redgrave started reshaping the world in her image, but apparently I was wrong.

'... big loud-mouthed Yanks ...' the cornet-player was rambling on.

'What's his name?' I asked the woman.

'Phillip Jason.'

That didn't sound real either, a throwback to the days when actors were called Gaylord and Bransby. I told the barmaid to get me one of whatever it was Jason drank.

'... no manners, think they own the world ...' mumbled in my ear.

'Have a drink Mr. Jason,' I said. 'Miss Williams still with you?'

'What, oh, thank you, dear,' the corduroy jacket said. He picked up the glass which gleamed pinkly. 'Miss who?'

'Miss Williams. B.J. Williams, from Radio Humberside. She came here to talk to you.'

'... and that suit and hat. Jesus, whoever made that suit ...'

'Not me, dear. I think I know who you mean though. Dark hair, legs all the way up,' Jason tittered like a schoolgirl.

'You haven't seen her today?'

'No, should I have done?'

'... and all those tattoos, ridiculous. One or two maybe alright but all over ...'

'I thought she was coming here to meet you

78

today,' I said.

'Not me, dear. Sorry. Friend of yours is she?' The question came out archly and I nodded my head hastily. 'Pity,' he said and fluttered his eyelashes at me.

'Thanks,' I said hurriedly and swallowed the rest of my drink and turned to the cornet-player who was still rumbling away about the big man who had spoiled his evening. Even a duff, part-time, cornet-player was safer ground than getting embroiled with the Phillip Jasons of this world.

'Have another pint?' I asked him.

He shook his head. 'No, time to get back and pull them into line.'

I turned my attention to the band. He was right, by his standards they were out of line. The trumpet player who was sitting-in his place was rippling through a series of chords the cornet-player probably hadn't known existed. The tune was 'Round Midnight which was about fifty years ahead of the cornet-player's musical mentality. The trumpet solo was followed by one from a young trombone player I hadn't seen around before. He was good, very good, and the three choruses he played before he was nudged out by an indifferent altoist made the others sound like what they really were.

My cornet-playing companion wandered back towards the band and left me with Jason.

'Time for another?' he asked me.

79

'Another time,' I said.

'Anytime at all, dear,' he said. 'Absolutely any time.'

I caught the barmaid's eye. She was trying her best not to fall about and I suppose the mild panic I was displaying was amusing to her. I grinned at her and she winked back. I looked a little more closely. Not in B.J. Williams' class maybe, but no parrot either. I returned her wink and made a mental note to call back and see her another time.

I walked towards the Cortina, trying to work out what the morning's events added up to. If B.J. Williams hadn't come to the theatre early that morning to talk to the producer then she must have been there for one thing only, to see me. Somehow she had known I was there and had proceeded to offer herself for a morning's roll in the hay. It didn't make a lot of sense. I'm not knocking my own ability in that area, I can make my point better than most, but I wasn't fooling myself into thinking that women, particularly women in B.J.'s class, would line up for it. Certainly not at some ungodly hour in the morning. So, she'd presented herself to me, but why?

I remembered the telephone call that she seemed to have been making while I showered. Getting instructions maybe? No, more likely giving them, telling someone that I was out of the way and would be for some time. That was why she'd taken my clothes into the bedroom, there was no chance, once I got in there wearing nothing but a towel, that I would leave. Not with her stretched out on the bed in open invitation.

Then there was the other telephone call, the one she didn't answer. That was someone calling her back to say that whatever was being done, had been done. Which would account for the fact that immediately afterwards she lost interest in me and gave me the rush.

All very interesting, and very, very much a matter of guesswork. But it was easily settled. If someone wanted me out of the way for an hour or two it could be for only one reason.

I reached the car and found I hadn't escaped the Demon Traffic Warden. I unglued the ticket from the windscreen and thought about throwing it away but then thought better of it. A six pound traffic fine was one thing, throwing litter on the road was very probably an offence punishable by deportation.

It took me less than two minutes to get home. I went up the stairs quickly and quietly although I was sure no-one would be there.

I was right on both counts. First, nobody was there and second, someone had turned over the room with a thoroughness that had to be seen to be believed. They'd even taken up the floorboards.

I sat down in the middle of it all and thought

about what I would do next if I happened to be in their boots. I didn't much like the answer I came up with.

CHAPTER SIX

The search of my room having failed to produce what they were looking for, either the diamonds or the money or both, there seemed little doubt that the next thing the opposition would do would be to lean on me. Hard.

I slid smartly down to Carole's room, knocked, got no reply and did things to her door lock with a little plastic calendar. An internationally-known motor car tyre manufacturer provided them by the million and would, doubtless, have been shocked to learn that they could be used for things other than merely finding out what day it was.

I had a quick look round. As far as I could see they hadn't searched her room which seemed to be an indication that they weren't perfect. I went out and down the stairs, into the Cortina and away without any trouble. Maybe it was all in my mind. Like hell it was.

I stopped at the first telephone kiosk I came to, found the phone had been vandalised and stopped at two more before I found one that still worked.

I called Doris Perkins and she came to the telephone sounding as if she'd just baked loaves for the five thousand.

'It's me, Johnny,' I told her.

'I've been trying to get you.'

'Oh?'

'He's back.'

'Good, I'll be there in ten minutes.'

'No you won't. He's worn out, poor love. He's sleeping. Come tonight. Sevenish. You can eat with us.'

I thought about that. It was an attractive idea. 'Sorry,' I said. 'I think I'll be busy until later. About eight thirty or nine.'

'He'll be in the Hastings by then.'

'Right, tell him I'll see him there.'

'Alright, love.'

'Doris, listen, there's a parcel coming for me. It's coming to your house. I didn't want it at Park Street. It's, er, quite valuable.' I didn't like lying to her.

'I'm not surprised you don't trust the kind of people who live in a place like that.'

I lived in a place like that, but I didn't say so. I knew what she meant. 'Put it somewhere safe for me, will you? I won't want it for quite a while.' Not until the dust settled, or I'd spent the rest of the hundred I'd taken out of the package.

She told me she would and I put down the

telephone, relieved that I had covered a loose end and that I would have a chance to talk to Big Eric soon.

I took a short drive round a few back streets until I was sure I didn't have company then headed for somewhere I could leave the car while I made a couple of calls on foot.

I reached the Royal Infirmary just in time to see the afternoon visitors swarm in, brandishing bunches of flowers and bottles of Lucozade like twentieth century charms to ward off evil spirits. I filtered quietly into Casualty and hung about until I spotted a likely-looking young nurse with a figure that was very nearly too big for her uniform. When she went out I followed her into the corridor and turned on the charm I save for special occasions.

She hadn't been on duty the night I had dropped Claude Jenks in Ferensway but she told me the name of a friend who had. I managed to prise the friend's name and address out of her and in return I promised to do nothing to the friend I wouldn't be able to repeat with her when her next day off came round.

I went out to find the rain had started and it looked as if it would stay that way. I resisted the impulse to walk back to where I had left the car. I wanted to attract as little attention as possible and walking in the wet streets in my shabby gear I was just any other down-at-heel deadbeat. My car, readily identifiable by the rust patches and half-hearted attempts to fill in the holes with fibre-glass, would have made me more noticeable than I wanted to be at that moment.

The off-duty nurse shared a flat with three other nurses just around the corner in Great Portland Street. She came to the door after I'd banged and kicked for several minutes. I told her my name and the name of her friend who'd given me her address and after a while she reluctantly let me in. Maybe she'd been dreaming about the Boston Strangler.

'Tuesday night,' I said, when we were inside and sitting down. 'You were on duty all night?'

'Yes, ten until eight.'

'Do you remember a man being brought in, he was big, American and covered in tattoos.'

The tattoos lit the lamp for her. 'Him,' she said. 'Yes, what a sight. Covered he was.'

I thought about my last sight of him. 'Yes, he was.'

'His name was Jenkins or Jenks or something like that.'

'Yes. Who brought him in?'

She thought for a moment. 'An ambulance I think.'

'How did he die?'

'Coronary.'

'You're sure?'

'I think so. Why?'

I ignored her question. 'What about the

85

police. Were they involved?'

'There was a constable there, came in at the same time as the ambulance. I think he'd found him in the street.'

'No other policemen?'

'One came later, a big man, bigger than the tattooed man. An inspector, I think.'

'I know him. What time was all this?'

'I hadn't been on duty long, maybe ten thirty or eleven, no later than that.' So Claude Jenks had had his heart attack, if that's what it was, very shortly after I'd dropped him off. 'Why are you asking all these questions?' the nurse asked me.

'I did a job for him,' I lied. 'He owed me some money and I wanted to know who to see about it.'

'The big policeman took away all his belongings.'

'Did you see them?'

'No, one of the orderlies dealt with that.'

I nodded and thought hard. I couldn't think of anything else I could ask. 'Thank you,' I said.

'Can I go back to bed now?' she asked.

There wasn't an invitation in the words. My luck had run out for the day which was probably as well. My leg was beginning to ache and I wasn't sure whether it was the wet weather or the exceptional treatment it had been given in B.J. Williams' bed.

'Yes,' I said. 'Go back to bed, I'm sorry to

have bothered you.'

She let me out and I heard the lock turn behind me.

I hiked off down the road towards the police station. They seemed to have lost interest in me which meant that if I wanted to learn anything I would have to go to them, however reluctant I might feel about such action.

Not knowing the big policeman's name didn't delay matters very much. The young constable at the reception desk, looking all of fourteen years old, repressed a grin when I gave my description of the big, bear-like man.

'Detective Inspector Gostelow,' he told me. 'I'll see if he's in. What's your name?'

I told him and he looked down his list for Gostelow's internal number, dialled it and mumbled into the telephone for a few seconds. 'He'll be down in a couple of minutes,' he told me. 'Wait there.'

I looked round. There, was one of four chairs placed in front of the plate glass windows that faced onto the gardens where any casual passer-by could see me waiting to tell all to the law. Fortunately the chairs had their backs to the windows and I sat in one of them and tried to be inconspicuous.

Gostelow's couple of minutes turned out to be nearer ten and I watched people coming and going. I noticed that the inner set of glass doors could not be opened from the outside until the fourteen year old constable pressed a button. Harder to get in than to get out. Sign of the times, I suppose.

When Gostelow appeared he let me in through one of the doors and preceded me down the corridor, trying various doors until he found a room that wasn't occupied.

He sat on the corner of a desk and pointed at a chair. 'Sit,' he said. I sat. 'Well?'

'Claude Jenks,' I said.

He looked momentarily puzzled before comprehension dawned. That little hesitation told me several things. One was that Gostelow was a busy man and had other things on his mind, which didn't surprise me. The other was that Jenks had very probably really died from a heart attack and that my previous interview with Gostelow had been a result of the inspector filling in time until he got the post-mortem results.

'What about him?' he asked.

'I wondered if you knew where I could reach his business partners.'

'Why should I know?'

'You knew about me, I assume he had a diary or a notebook or something of the sort. If my name was in it then probably theirs were too.'

He looked at me in silence.

I felt impelled to stammer on. 'If I knew who they were I might be able to get work from them, the same job, whatever it was that he . . .'

I stumbled to a stop.

Gostelow looked at me silently for a few more moments then he seemed to take pity on me. 'Okay,' he said. 'Wait here.'

He was gone another five minutes during which time the door opened twice and faces peered round. It seemed everybody was looking for a free office. Undermanned or not, they were suffering from lack of space.

When Gostelow came back he had a large manilla envelope in his big hands. He fished a small grey-blue notebook out of the envelope and flicked through it. He stopped at one page and showed it to me. My name and the number of the telephone on the second-floor landing were written on the page in spidery, flowing writing.

'That's how we came looking for you,' he volunteered. 'Thought you might be able to identify him.'

'That was before you knew how he'd died,' I said, just to show how clever I was.

He grinned at me. 'Smart boy.' He turned a couple more pages then dropped the notebook back into the envelope, fished around and came up with another book. This one was a diary. He flicked through that and then shook his head. 'Nothing there,' he said. 'Sorry.'

'So am I,' I said. 'I needed the work.'

'Whatever it was?'

I didn't miss the inflection, he had stopped

playing friends and was back to being a policeman again.

'Within reason,' I said.

He thought about that. 'Yes, you probably mean it. As far as we know you haven't done anything that would interest us. Yet. It's just the friends you keep that worries us.' He reached out and opened the door. I stood up and went out into the corridor.

He escorted me to the main doors, he didn't want me to get lost on the way out and accidentally end up in the cells.

I walked through the drizzle and formed several conclusions that had nothing to do with the diamonds, the money or the tattooed man. One was that I was wet and cold and getting scruffier by the minute. Another was that walking wasn't doing as much harm to my dodgy leg as I had expected. Maybe the doctors had been right after all.

I went into C & A and treated myself to a pair of slacks, a shirt and an anorak, two sizes too big but which fitted over my leather jacket. I insisted on wearing my purchases while the assistant carefully packed my old stuff. I let her keep the yellow, red and purple shirt, which didn't seem to please her all that much.

Then I went into the station and treated myself to several cups of coffee and a plateful of sugary doughnuts. By the time I'd finished those my brain was functioning on a more important level. One thing was fairly obvious. Whether or not he wanted me to think so, Gostelow was still interested in the case of the tattooed man. Pretending to go through the dead man's notebook and diary was just that, a pretence. He would know their contents backwards and if there had been anything in there that was of interest to me he wouldn't need to look. And if there had been he would've given up half his pension before showing it to me.

The act had been to make me think he valued my friendship and wanted to keep it. For what reason? There seemed to be only one. In some way, my crashing about, talking to people and generally making a nuisance of myself was benefiting a police investigation.

I couldn't imagine why but it seemed to suggest that Gostelow really did have tabs on me and even if the morose-looking man I'd seen hadn't been a copper then one was there, somewhere, lurking in the background, ready to leap out and take all the credit when the time was right. Hopefully he might also save me from a fate worse than death in the process. It was a comforting thought but try as I did, I couldn't see anyone around me who looked like a policeman.

I finished the last of the doughnuts and went out into the cold and the rain feeling less scruffy in my new clothes. I thought about the remains of the six thousand pounds and the diamonds.

When I got out of this tangle and knew for certain that Claude Jenks's friends were no longer interested in me, I would have a spending spree that would put some real clothes on my back. Not the tat I usually wore.

It was a nice feeling, but it didn't last long.

I went out of the rear station exit, crossed the road and went into a second-hand bookshop where I bought a dozen paperbacks of the right size. A few yards from the bookshop was a commercial stationers and from there I bought some sheets of brown paper and a large roll of Sellotape. Then I headed back to my car and went home, if that's what it was, to my room.

I made up twelve brown-paper packages that looked like the original package of diamonds but which felt softer as I didn't have any tin boxes.

I sneaked another look into Carole's room, then went out and started laying a few false trails. It took me some hours and by the time I had finished it was almost eight-thirty and I went down to the Hastings to meet Big Eric.

CHAPTER SEVEN

Big Eric was sitting on a high stool by the bar, looking for all the world like a garden gnome and using both hands to control the pint of bitter he was busily drinking.

92

I told the barman to pour another one and get me a scotch and Big Eric, recognising my voice, turned round and grinned broadly at me, displaying a wide expanse of pink gum.

'Now then Eric old lad,' I said. 'How are you keeping, you old rogue?'

He turned up a thumb to indicate all was well in his world.

'Still with the circus?'

Again the thumb.

I sipped at the scotch and thought out the questions I would need to ask, bearing in mind he was limited in what he could convey to me without words.

'I met someone the other day,' I said quietly. I didn't think anyone else in the pub would be interested but there was no point in being careless. 'American, roughly late forties, maybe fifty. Big, about six, six one. Weight, oh, say two hundred and fifty pounds. Covered in tattoos. All kinds; pictures of lions, dragons, eagles.' I screwed up my eyes, remembering the body on the trolley. 'Scrolls, shields, fishes. All colours, green and red, blue and black.' I stopped and let him think about that for a moment. 'Any ideas?' I asked, eventually.

He finished off his pint and reached for the one I had bought. One swallow took a third of that one and he wiped his hand across his mouth and nodded at me.

I felt a slight quickening of my pulse. 'The

93

name he was using was Jenks, Claude Jenks.'

Big Eric shook his head at that.

'Do you know his real name?'

A nod.

That gave me a problem because Big Eric had never got around to learning how to read or write. I thought about things for a moment and came to the conclusion it didn't really matter all that much.

'Where did you know him? Circus?'

A shake of the head.

'Halls?'

A shake.

'Fairground?'

A grin and a nod.

'This country?'

A nod and a shake.

'Here and abroad?'

A nod.

'America?'

A nod. I knew that he had been to America about ten or more years before.

'What was he? A sideshow? The Tattooed Man?'

A nod that wasn't quite a nod.

'Something else as well?'

A nod.

I felt weary, talking to Big Eric tended to be something of a strain. I ordered more drinks and looked around the room at the other early evening customers. I didn't see any familiar faces, not that I'd been in there for years but it was something of a relief to see none of my more recent acquaintances had put in an appearance. Again I didn't see anyone who looked at all like a policeman, but then, come to think of it, neither had Gostelow the big bear, or the fourteen year old policeman at the headquarters' reception desk.

I turned back to Big Eric who was clutching his latest pint in both hands. 'When did you last see him?'

He stood his glass on the bar and held up one hand, fingers outstretched, and showed one finger of the other hand.

'Six years?'

No, that wasn't right.

'Six months?'

That wasn't right either.

'Six weeks?' My voice sounded faintly incredulous, even to me.

Big Eric nodded.

Well, well, I thought. 'Where? Which town?'

He fumbled in his pocket and came up with a tattered diary that I'd seen before. To my certain knowledge he'd had it for fifteen years. He opened it and I caught a glimpse of the date. 1961. Well over fifteen years. He carried it with him as a personal phrase-book. Each page had written on it some phrase or other for when he was with people unaccustomed to his affliction and unwilling to spend time trying to understand him. He had memorised where each of the phrases came in the book and when the need arose he would pull it out, open it up, and point.

Now he opened it to the maps on the last few pages. He pointed.

'Bristol?'

A nod.

Now what had I got? Claude Jenks, or whatever his name was, had been in Bristol six weeks earlier. It didn't help.

Big Eric tapped my arm, pointed at my glass and floated a pound note across the bar. I finished my drink and called the barman down to us. In one corner of the room two young tearaways were getting heated over the early season showing of Hull City and their voices were about the only sounds in there. A big change from the other pubs I'd been into recently. I decided I preferred it that way. Maybe I was getting old.

I turned back to Big Eric. 'When you saw him in Bristol, did he have anyone with him? Friends? Other fair people?'

He thought about that and then nodded. He made a few gestures with his hands, the time-honoured wavy lines that signified a woman's body followed by a circle around his own face and a beaming smile. A woman, nice figure, pretty, very probably young too. It didn't help. I was beginning to think my hopes that Big Eric would be able to give me some useful information had been premature. Unless, I thought, there was something there I hadn't been able to connect up.

'Thanks a lot, Eric,' I told the little man. 'If you think of anything that might be of any help get Doris to ring me will you?'

He nodded and looked enquiringly at my glass but I shook my head. Instead, I bought a bottle of scotch, pushed it in my pocket and left him rapping on the counter with his already empty glass. It was a mystery where he put all the beer he drank. His capacity was greater than men of three or four times his bulk.

I went out to the car-park and unlocked the door of the Cortina. As I did so I heard rapid and not very soft footsteps on the asphalt behind me. Instinct took over and I hurriedly tried to get into the car but hands seized me and pulled me backwards. I hung on to the car for a few seconds but then a fist slammed into my back. All the breath went out of my body and I let go of the door. Some remote part of my brain told me that, although a fist had hit me, two hands were still holding and pulling at me. There were two of them.

Then I was spun around and a fist went into my stomach but it didn't hurt as much as I would have expected. Maybe it was the protection given by the new anorak on top of my leather jacket or maybe they were out for something other than a simple beating.

As if to confirm that I was thinking coherently, even though I was being held as tightly as a child might hold a rag-doll, a face was thrust close to mine.

'Where is it?' a voice said.

I shook my head and didn't say anything. A hand gripped my throat and squeezed, not too hard, but, like the blow to the stomach, there was no doubt that he wasn't hurting me because he didn't want to.

'Listen, Baxter, we don't want to hurt you ...' the voice trailed off leaving me in no doubt that nothing would give its owner greater pleasure than to do just that.

'What ...' I swallowed painfully and tried again. 'What do you want?'

'The package. Where is it?'

'Wh ... ?'

'Don't say what package or I might lose my temper.'

I was glad of the interruption. It probably saved me another thump in the stomach. 'I've hidden it,' I said quickly.

'Where?'

'In the glove compartment of an old Vauxhall Cresta. It's in a scrap-merchant's yard.'

'Go on.'

I told them where I'd hidden one of the dummy packages I'd made up that afternoon. They weren't sure, I could tell, but in the end

98

they believed me.

'Okay,' one of them said. He stepped back and I heard him whisper something to his mate. I steeled myself for a bashing but just then I heard shouting and footsteps clattering across the car-park. The two heavies ran for it and I fell back onto the hard surface and tried to stop shaking.

I heard a car start up and drive away at high speed. More hands took hold of me and helped me to my feet. I opened my eyes. It was one of the two tearaways who had been arguing about football.

'Anything broken?' he asked me.

'No, they didn't have time. Thanks.'

'That's what we're here for,' he said.

Before I could ask what that meant his mate came trotting back to us. 'They're away,' he said. 'I got the car number. I'll call in with it.'

He crossed to a car parked near mine, opened the door and in a moment I heard him speak.

'Police?' I said, to prove that my brain hadn't been damaged.

'Yes.'

'Inspector Gostelow's merry band?'

He nodded, unsure if he was supposed to tell me things like that. I turned to go towards my car and Big Eric materialised at my side. He gripped my arm and thrust an enquiring, concerned face into mine.

'I'm okay, mate,' I said. The policeman in the

car began to give a description of the men and their car and its number. I looked at Big Eric who was listening intently. He caught my look and from his expression I sensed that the information the policeman was giving meant more to him than it did to any of us.

I reached my car and dropped heavily onto the seat. I looked up at the policeman. 'Thanks,' I said. 'It's nice to know I've got friends.'

He grinned at me. 'Gostelow doesn't have friends,' he said. 'Remember that and you'll last a lot longer.'

The other policeman came back and joined his mate. 'Where are you going now?' he asked me.

There was no longer any need for deception on their part and I suspected he'd just been told to stay even closer. 'Home,' I said.

'Right, we'll follow you. Have a good night's rest and we'll see you in the morning.'

From his voice I could tell that Gostelow hadn't taken them too much into his confidence. They had no idea who I was or where I came on the social scale of police, villains and the general public.

I nodded. It seemed like a good idea. I looked at Big Eric who treated me to a wink and mimed that he would contact me when he knew something about the men who had attacked me. I had a feeling he might very well find them before the police did.

I drove away, gaining some pleasure from the knowledge that if the two heavies tried to break into the scrap-yard that night they would have the owner's half-wild Alsatian to contend with.

It was a nice thought. It almost made up for the punch in the back and the much heavier blow to my pride.

My room didn't look any better than usual, but it didn't look any worse either. I thought about preparing a meal but came to the conclusion that my heart wouldn't be in it and instead I made out a list, planning to spend some of the money on food. Having already spent some of it on clothes to protect me from the elements it wouldn't be a bad idea to buy something that would help prevent me from dying of starvation.

I had just written down, 'tins of beans—several' when I heard Carole come up the stairs. I went out on to the landing and called down to her and she came up the remaining flight of stairs and eagerly agreed to let me repay her hospitality of a few nights earlier. It was some time since I'd had a bottle of scotch to call my own and we made the most of it.

I'm not sure if there's a moral question involved when it comes to supplying booze to someone with a drink problem. Perhaps there is, but, as with most moral and ethical issues that come up in my life from time to time, I ignored it.

'What happened? You finally made a bet on a horse with four legs?'

We were in bed, more for warmth and comfort than for sex, although, the way I was beginning to feel, as the whisky anaesthetized the aches in my back and stomach, that would soon follow. There was no need to ask how Carole felt, her hands were conducting their almost automatic survey of my body.

'Something like that,' I said. There didn't seem to be any point in involving her any more than was necessary in my affairs.

'Anything to do with that job in the Midlands?'

'What job in the Midlands?'

'You told me you would be away for a few days.'

I'd forgotten. Which makes me a bad liar, a good memory being the first requisite. 'That fell through,' I said. 'This was a little deal I did with some scrap metal.'

'Oh.' She had lost interest but, having jolted me into remembering what I'd told her, I also remembered the rest of that particular conversation.

'Did you contact B.J. Williams?' I asked.

'Yes. It's a job, nothing much. A radio play.'

I waited but she didn't go on. 'You looked surprised, puzzled.'

'What? When?'

'When I told you she'd been to see you.'

'Oh, yes, well it's a long time since people came looking for me to offer me work.' She said it without bitterness.

'I suppose so,' I said, trying to think of some way to change the subject.

'Anyway, I thought she was still away.'

'Oh.' I reached down, hoisted the bottle off the floor and refilled our glasses.

'Thanks,' she said.

I moved slightly so that her free hand had more freedom of movement and very soon I forgot about my cares and woes and aches and pains while we used each other's bodies for our own private needs. That's all it was, a bodily function. I tried to remember if it had ever been anything other than that. Perhaps it had, but for the first time I could remember, I found myself making comparisons between Carole and other women. There wasn't much doubt that on nothing more than a sexual level she took some beating but there was a mindless intensity about her behaviour that made it impossible to think of sex with her as an act of love. I thought about the session with B.J. Williams and found the comparison unsatisfactory and wondered if a setting like B.J.'s flat would have made Carole seem better than she did in the cheap rooms we occupied. Obviously it would have helped, but then, I expect it would have helped anyone.

Unwillingly I found myself facing the conclusion that something else had crept into the feelings I had about B.J. Williams. I wasn't ready to put a name to it, at least not until that something else had been given time to either fade away or harden into reality. Whatever the eventual outcome, I had let the tall, long-legged radio producer get closer to me than I was ready to admit.

Emotional feelings apart there was no doubt that the physical side of sex with Carole was the same as always and, aided by the inner warmth of the scotch, I drifted into light sleep with her curled tightly in my arms. After a while I eased away from her, planning to turn out the light.

She stirred at my movement, opened her eyes and gazed at me without recognition for a split-second. Then she relaxed as if accepting that whatever else I might be, I wasn't a threat to her.

'Okay?' I asked.

'Sure.'

'Another drink?'

'Not now.'

I didn't press her. She opened her eyes and looked at me carefully.

'*Are* you okay?' I asked.

'Of course, why shouldn't I be?'

'No reason, it's ...'

'It's just that I don't often refuse a drink.'

'That isn't what I was going to say.'

'I'm sorry, Johnny, it's just that ...' Her voice trailed away and I was surprised to see tears glisten in her eyes.

'What's wrong? Tell me.'

'I . . . no, it's just that a friend of mine, a very good friend died recently and I . . . I haven't all that many friends left.' There was no self-pity in her voice.

'There's still me,' I said trying to sound more sincere than I felt.

She smiled a little at that and brushed at her eyes. 'Until it becomes a responsibility,' she said quietly.

'What does that mean?'

'It means you're not the type to take on responsibilities, not your own and certainly not those of others.'

I felt a tiny twinge of irritation. It always annoyed me when people, women in particular, turned into amateur psychologists. Then I buried the feeling of annoyance because, as far as Carole was concerned, it was unjustified.

Instead, I changed the subject. Something had been nagging at me since the conversation we'd had before sex and sleep had interrupted.

'You said B.J. Williams had been away. Where, do you know?'

'She's been on a three month exchange with another local radio station.'

'Where?' I asked, but I had a feeling I already knew the answer.

'Bristol,' she said.

CHAPTER EIGHT

I woke up as Carole climbed out of bed and began to gather her clothes together.

'What time is it?' I asked.

'Ten.'

The heavy-weights would have had time to find that I had misled them about the package at the scrap-yard and, depending on the mood the Alsatian had been in, they would be less than pleased with me.

Apart from getting out of their way, there were a few other things I needed to do, like finding out precisely what B.J. Williams and Inspector Gostelow were up to. If I was to keep my hands on the diamonds and the money, and I intended doing both, my need to find out who they really belonged to was pressing. I had to know who to avoid if I wanted to stay in one piece.

I scrambled out of bed, gasping as the cold air hit me. That was something else I would do when it was safe to spend the money; find a better place to live and one where there was some form of heating other than the one-bar electric fire that worked when I put coins in the meter, and not always then.

As I dressed, Carole went out and I heard her go into the bathroom on her floor. By the time I was fully dressed I could hear the sound of water as she ran her bath. I slid down the stairs and did things to her lock with my plastic calendar.

In her room I went quickly through the things I had left there for safety. When I was happy that all was well I let myself out and went on down the stairs to face another cold, bleak, morning.

I checked that my protectors from the previous night were on duty and gave them a wave to show that I hadn't been murdered in my bed. I walked round to the garage thinking about Gostelow. Whatever devious game he was playing I was certain that he hadn't put two men to watch me because he valued my skin. He knew, I guessed, something more than he had revealed and was using me as bait, like a tethered goat in tiger country. If that was the case then I reckoned I needed to know a little more about what he knew. The problem was, how to get the information without letting him know just how involved I really was.

Doing my best to avoid the worst of the potholes, I drove into the street and saw Big Eric's lorry. It was unmistakable, apart from the brightly painted bodywork with pictures of lions and elephants and the name of the circus he worked for, it looked as if it was driving itself. Big Eric's head was barely visible as he peered over the steering wheel. That meant he was sitting down, something he didn't often do in the lorry, most of the time he stood up. He must have been feeling weary that morning. Sitting down presented him with a few problems. One was being unable to see very much out of the windscreen, the other was being unable to reach the pedals. In the past he had overcome the second problem by fitting wooden blocks to them, the way small boys sometimes fit them to bicycle pedals. He didn't do it now because he'd been done for driving with blocks. I'm not sure how they'd managed to dream up a charge but it hadn't stuck. The magistrate, himself no giant, had thrown the case out but Big Eric wasn't one to push his luck. So far no-one had managed to work out if standing up to drive was a contravention of any law and until they did that was the way he preferred to drive.

He stopped and so did I and climbed out of the Cortina, opened the door of the lorry and scrambled up into the cab.

'Morning, Eric. Everything okay?'

I got a thumbs-up sign. Then he frowned in concern and pointed at me, raising his eyebrows as he did so.

'Yes, fine, thanks,' I told him. 'My back still hurts, but nothing to worry about.'

He nodded and his smile came back.

'The police are still here,' I said, pointing at the car parked a short distance away.

He glanced at them and nodded then did a mime of one of them talking on the radio.

'You recognised the descriptions?'

He nodded.

'Locals?'

A shake.

I pulled a thought out of the air. 'Bristol?'

A nod.

I didn't know what I was getting but at least I was starting to tie a few people together; first the dead man, Claude Jenks, then B.J. Williams, now the heavy mob, all together in Bristol a few weeks earlier and now all here in Hull.

'At a fair?' I asked.

A nod.

'Same place as the tattooed man?'

That was right too. I thought about Big Eric's description of Jenks' companion, a pretty girl with a nice figure. I described B.J. to him but got an emphatic shake of the head. So much for that.

I turned to more immediate matters and asked him if the two men from last night were connected with the fair that would be almost completely assembled in Hull, ready for the opening next day.

I got a nod for that.

'Are they there now?'

Yes, apparently they were.

'I think I'd better take a look,' I told him. 'Can you take me in this? It'll be less conspicuous than if I go in my car.' Less conspicuous in a bright red lorry with wild animals painted all over it!

He grinned and gave me a thumbs-up. I clambered down and locked the Cortina then climbed back up into his cab again and we were off to the fair.

A fair that size can't make do with a few scraps of wasteland. It needs a large permanent site and the city council provided one, about a mile from where I lived. A few acres of land along the eastern side of Walton Street. The street ran between two main roads leading from the city centre and the houses along the other side of it were old, depressingly seedy, turn-of-the-century, buildings held together by force of habit. A pub at each end of the street, a few broken down shops and a couple of used car lots made it almost uniformly grim during fifty-one weeks in every year.

During the other week it was as if some good fairy had waved a magic wand over it. The open space on the other side of the street is covered in a mass of stalls and caravans, tents and rides, trailers and sideshows. There are huge, lorry-mounted generators to supply the electricity needed to operate the machinery and to provide the tens of thousands of coloured lights that turn the whole place into a child's idea of fairyland.

The fair doesn't confine itself just to the open space but spreads up and down Walton Street, encroaching into the gardens of the seedy houses, an encroachment for which the owners

110

of the houses are handsomely recompensed by the stall-holders who need the space.

When Big Eric turned into the northern end of the street there was a hive-like mass of people frantically finishing off preparations for the bigger attractions that had been arriving over the past few days; the Big Wheel and the Dodgems, the Shamrock and the Octopus, and of course the circus. There were still a few spaces left for late arrivals who still had the rest of Friday to set-up.

Eric drove onto the black ash-covered surface, a surface that would turn, when it rained, into a black sludge. This was almost an inevitability as far as Hull Fair was concerned. He parked behind the circus tent and looked at me enquiringly.

'Show me where they hang out,' I said.

He nodded and scrambled agilely down from the cab.

I got down with less agility and followed him as he scurried along between rows of penny-rolling booths and air-rifle stalls. I kept my eyes open for familiar faces but didn't see any. I didn't even see my two guardian angels but I confidently expected they wouldn't be far away.

Big Eric stopped abruptly and I almost cannoned into him. He pointed at a large, opulent, caravan.

'There?'

He nodded.

'Who owns it?'

He made a complicated mime that started with a movement of his hands like a goalkeeper handling a football, followed by bending his head and shading his eyes with both hands as he peered downwards.

The caravan and its location on the fairground helped. 'A fortune-teller?'

I got an approving beam for that. I felt quite pleased about it myself.

'Thanks,' I said. 'Look, you'd better float off. I'll take it from here.'

He didn't think too much of that I could tell, but he accepted that if I said it was my business then it probably was. He disappeared between a coconut shy, something I thought had disappeared with trolley-buses and rock salt, and a try-your-strength machine.

I had another look around for the two young policemen but I still couldn't see them. I tried to recall if I'd noticed them following us down the road but I couldn't. I had a momentary qualm but then I shrugged it off. I'd received a thumping when they were watching me so their presence didn't seem to make very much difference one way or the other.

I wandered up to the big caravan and did one complete lap around it. All the curtains were pulled across and I couldn't hear any sounds from inside but there was a lot of noise going on all around me so that didn't mean a lot.

I decided that my chances of being jumped in broad daylight were slim, so I began to walk up to the door to knock.

At that moment I saw the door handle start to turn and I ducked smartly around the end of the caravan and waited a few seconds before cautiously sneaking a look around the corner.

I hadn't seen the faces of the two men the night before but the two who came down the steps resembled the description the policeman had radioed in after the fracas in the car-park at the Hastings. One of them turned and looked back up at the door they had just left by.

'There'll be no problems. Even if the owner's a friend of his we can find an excuse to look in the car he said he'd hidden it in.'

I watched them go, the one who'd spoken had a bandage on his left hand. While I had no way of knowing if he'd been wearing it the night before, I took a guess that they had tried to get into the scrap-yard during the night and had been chased out by the Alsatian.

I followed them a short distance trying to decide whether I would gain more by following them than by going back to the caravan. Then I felt a hand on my arm and I spun round ready for a fight. It was one of the policemen.

'Okay, mate,' he said. 'Relax. We're on your side, remember.'

'You just aged me,' I said.

'That them?' he jerked his thumb after the

113

two men.

'Yes.'

'Any idea where they came from?'

'No,' I lied, an idea forming in my mind.

'And no idea where they're going?'

'Not a clue.' I was getting good at it.

'Okay, I think I'll come with you.'

'With me?'

'You were following them.'

'Yes, but if you are there's no need for me as well. Where's your mate?'

'Back at the ranch.'

'I'll leave you to it, then.'

'What are you going to do?' he said suspiciously.

'I'm a working man,' I said. 'I might be able to pick up some work around here.'

He glanced after the two men who had reached the edge of the fairground and were walking north up Walton Street. He was getting worried in case he lost them.

'Don't try anything fancy,' he said.

'Who me?' I said.

He treated me to a glare and hurried after the two men and I stood and watched him go.

When he was too far away to see where I went, if he happened to look back and change his mind, I wandered casually back towards the fortune-teller's caravan.

There didn't seem any point in hanging about where too many people could see me, so I went straight up the steps, opened the door and went in.

Inside, the caravan was furnished and decorated more lavishly than most houses. Although modern there was an old-fashioned air to it, created by the pictures, mostly photographs, that lined every wall and were also in small frames dotted about on the flat surfaces that were not already covered in small Capo di Monti figures. I stood for a second, uncertain what to do, having expected to see someone there. Then a curtain at the far end of the caravan moved and a woman appeared.

She stopped in her tracks when she saw me.

'Who are you?' she asked.

'I'm here about the consignment,' I said.

She was about forty, maybe a little older, dark-complexioned with her hair pulled back from her forehead by a bright, multi-coloured silk square. She was wearing heavy earrings, rings and bracelets and altogether looked like everyone's popular conception of a gypsy fortune-teller. Her eyes had narrowed at my opening remark and there was a long silence while we studied each other.

'What consignment?' she said eventually.

I shrugged my shoulders. 'If you don't know then I've come to the wrong place,' I said and turned away.

'Wait.' She snapped out the one word and I stopped but didn't turn round. 'You're Baxter,'

115

she said after a moment or two.

I turned round then and grinned at her. 'If I am, does that explain what the consignment is?'

She nodded slowly. 'It does.'

'Right then, let's talk.'

'What about?'

'I would've thought that was obvious,' I said. 'You want it back don't you? And they're not going to find it,' I added.

For the briefest instant of time something flashed in her eyes and then she nodded. 'Of course,' she agreed.

'What's it worth to get it back?' I said.

'What do you think?'

I put on my honest-as-the-day-is-long face. 'I don't know very much about this kind of thing. Not my league really.'

'So you're open to offers?'

'Yes, but I have a nose for people who are trying to take me for a ride.'

'I'll have a talk with someone.'

I nodded at the door. 'Not those two?'

Her face told me the answer before she spoke. 'Those idiots? No, not them.'

'Who then?'

Her face closed up again. 'No-one you need know.'

'How long before you have an answer?'

'This time tomorrow.'

'Where?'

'Here.'

I thought for a moment. 'Make it the afternoon, about five.' There would be a lot of people around then, thousands of them, swarming all over the place.

'I'll be busy,' she said. 'I have a living to earn.'

Which confirmed that she wasn't the top of the heap. 'Don't we all, five o'clock I said and that's what I meant.' I went out of the caravan without waiting for her reply.

I walked towards the circus tent looking for Big Eric. I couldn't see him anywhere although his red lorry was where he had left it. I pushed open a flap in the tent wall and went inside. There was a thick, heady smell that combined canvas with grease and oil and the accumulated reminders of years and years of penned-in animal acts.

Two men were coming towards me, one my height, the other shorter and heavy-set. They looked slightly out of place there, the tall one particularly, dressed as he was in a dark business suit. It occurred to me that he might be one of the owners and anyway they both looked as if they knew their way about so I stopped them and spoke to the tall one. 'Have you seen Big Eric?'

The tall man had a beaky nose, almost invisible lips and dark, deep set eyes that gave him a vague appearance of how one imagined Sherlock Holmes should have looked. An effect slightly spoiled by the fact that this man had very little hair, what there was curled long and black over his ears, the top of his head was bald and tanned. The smooth high dome rose up to give an impression of an exceptionally high, intelligent forehead.

'Who shall I say wants him?' the man asked me, a slight accent softening his words.

'I'm a friend of his, tell him it's Johnny.'

Bald eagle's eyes flickered towards his companion and he nodded slightly. It occurred to me that he didn't really look like a man who would own a circus. The other man, however, didn't look at all out of place. He was short and chunky and had thick, mottled hair that seemed to sprout, not just from his scalp but also from his cheeks and nostrils and eyebrows. The thick eyebrows jutted forward making it almost impossible to determine the colour of his eyes, but they were sufficiently visible to let me see a glint that seemed oddly out of place until I added the glint to his companion's nod. I started to back away but I was too late, much too late. Before I had moved a couple of inches the smaller man hit me in the stomach. By comparison the blow of the previous evening was nothing more than a love-tap. I doubled up, bile forcing itself up into my throat as I tried to pull air back into my lungs. I saw the short man's knee coming up and there was nothing I could do but turn my head to one side so that he missed flattening my nose and hit my left cheek instead. I went over backwards, rolled away to one side and started to scramble to my feet, either to fight back or run for it, whichever seemed the most sensible course of action. At that moment the latter had most votes but I didn't get the chance to develop either idea as a heavy boot swept my legs from under me and I went down again.

'Hold him,' the tall man said in his soft voice and I felt a knee come down onto my neck, trapping me like a pinned beetle. I opened my eyes and saw a dark-clad pair of legs come into my view. They moved slightly as their owner crouched so that he could talk quietly to me.

'Alright, Baxter, tell us where you've hidden the package.'

I found myself taking the trouble to identify the accent. It was Irish, faint and softly pleasant. It didn't suit the tall man's austere appearance and what was happening to me. He sounded as if he should be using the voice to sing songs about mountains and rivers, not to ask questions about stolen diamonds while his hairy little friend was doing his best to separate my head from my body.

I tried to swallow and couldn't. I felt my face swelling with the pressure against my neck. I made a few helpless choking noises and the tall man took pity on me.

'Let him speak,' he told his friend and he

made it sound as if he was doing me a favour.

The leg on my neck moved fractionally and I managed to pull in a painful lungful of air. 'What are you talking about?' I said.

'Oh dear,' the soft voice said, politely. I saw his legs straighten and then move out of my sight. It wasn't more than a second or two before I knew where he'd moved to and why. The bald-headed man showed me that soft pleasant voice or not he wasn't there for amusement. He kicked me in the side, on the rib cage, just above the kidneys. I would have screamed if his partner hadn't re-applied pressure to my neck, effectively cutting off air, blood and whatever else goes up and down there.

I closed my eyes and tried to stop myself vomiting because in the position I was in it didn't seem like a very good idea. Everything turned red and then I opened my eyes again to find the red glow didn't completely disappear but it did fade enough to let me see that bald-eagle's legs were back in view again.

'You're out of your league, Baxter. In fact, everything about this is out of your league. Now, don't give me any nonsense such as—what package? We know you have them and we know how you laid your hands on them.'

I felt the leg on my neck ease fractionally again and I spat out some accumulated liquid. 'Okay,' I said. 'Public library. On the first floor, shelves on the left inside the double doors. There's a long row of telephone directories of American cities. It's pushed in behind them. Extreme right-hand end.'

There was a long silence while they decided whether I'd really hidden a package there.

'Okay,' the voice said. 'That takes care of one package. What about the other?'

'There's a music shop in Savile Street. The package is at the back of a rack of military marches in the record department.'

'You take big risks with other people's money,' the voice said softly, disbelievingly.

'The packages are addressed to me and they've got stamps on them ready for posting. If anyone found them the chances are they'd drop them in a post-box. Most people are honest.'

'You'd better be telling the truth, Baxter. If this is your idea of a joke you'll find I don't have a very well-developed sense of humour.'

'It's true,' I said.

There was a long silence and from somewhere not very far away I heard a sound that could have been a lion roaring. It didn't seem real but then neither did what was happening to me.

Suddenly the knee was released from my neck and I heard soft footsteps walking away. I stayed where I was for a few seconds and then started to get up. As I did so I realised I had heard the footsteps of only one person. I started to turn my head but something hit me hard, very hard at the back of my left ear and I floated downwards again with a roaring in my head that could have been the lion again but probably wasn't.

CHAPTER NINE

I struggled up out of a pit filled with bright red lions driving purple and pink lorries over my chest and neck. I could hear a voice talking a million miles away and eventually I managed to make out some words.

'The ambulance is here,' it said. I felt hands lift me and then I was floating gently through the air and I risked opening my eyes. I was on a stretcher and trotting alongside me was Big Eric. He saw my eyes were open and he tried a half smile that made me want to laugh, but I didn't. I had the distinct feeling that if I did it would very probably do me more harm than good.

The ambulance didn't take long to get me to the Royal Infirmary and with Big Eric ensuring the doctors didn't screw up my care and treatment, I was soon sitting up in a curtained cubicle in Casualty trying to decide whether I would live long enough to spend the money I was taking such risks to keep. I thought the odds against me were increasing with every hour that passed.

Apart from the bruises and, now, two cracked ribs, I'd collected some interesting information and I was learning things. For a start I now knew I didn't have just one mob after me, I had two. The two men from the car-park of the pub and the fortune-teller, were one team; the two men who had worked me over in the circus tent were another. It didn't take a genius to work out who was who. The flicker in the eyes of the fortune-teller, when I'd asked her if she wanted the package back, had been surprise. Surprise that I appeared to think the package had been hers in the first place. Also, both she and her heavies had talked about one package which meant they knew about the diamonds but not about the package of twenty-pound notes.

The other two knew about the diamonds and they knew about the money. That seemed to put them into the same team as Claude Jenks. They knew what they were after and they knew how I'd fallen into it all. The only thing they didn't know was where I'd hidden either the diamonds or the money and it wouldn't take them long to discover they were not where I'd told them to look.

I wondered about the casual way they had left me alone after the beating. They didn't appear to be unprofessional but that seemed careless, unless they were totally confident they could pick me up again whenever they felt like it. I didn't like the thought of that.

I tried to work out what my next move should be. At the back of my mind I'd always had a sneaking thought that an easy way out would be to try to sell the diamonds back to their owners, hence my approach to the fortune-teller. That now seemed less than clever in the light of the casually violent behaviour of the two men. If they thought I was trying a stunt like that they might very well decide to beat the truth out of me. I had a feeling they would very probably succeed in any such attempt.

It seemed the time had arrived for me to do something positive. The only positive thing I could think of was to make it clear to everyone, except the police, that I had the stones and then, just as clearly, let them think I had lost them. It wouldn't work if I simply told them I had lost the stones, they had to *see* me lose them. To be accurate, they had to *think* they were seeing me lose them. A tiny germ of an idea began to form, not much, but I began to feel a little better.

The curtain of the cubicle flicked to one side and I started up, expecting the worst, but it was a nurse and I relaxed again.

'Hello,' she said, as if she knew me.

I looked at her more closely. It was the nurse I'd visited to ask how the tattooed man had died.

'Hello,' I said and grinned at her. 'I didn't recognise you with your clothes on.'

124

She turned pink and came into the cubicle, closing the curtain behind her.

'Did you get what you wanted from the police?' she asked.

I dredged my memory for the lie I had told her. 'No,' I said.

'He must've owed money to a lot of people.'

'Oh.'

'Yes, apart from you, two others were enquiring about him.'

'Who were they?'

'I don't know their names.'

'Can you describe them?'

'One was a man. Just ordinary. Pudgy, but ordinary.'

That helped a lot but as I didn't want to offend her I didn't say so. Instead I said, 'What about the other one?'

'A woman. She was nice, very attractive.' There was a touch of longing in her voice and I looked at her carefully. She was really quite plain.

'Can you describe her?' I asked.

She did and this time her description was much better. It was B.J. Williams. That gave me something else to think about. 'Were they together?'

'No.'

'Can I go?' I asked, after a moment.

She glanced at a clipboard of papers covered in indecipherable scrawl. 'I expect so. I'll have a word with the doctor.'

She was gone a couple of minutes and then came back and told me to report back in a week and to take things easy in the meantime.

I started off down the corridor but she called out to me. 'My friend said, if I saw you again, I was to give you her name and address.'

'Which friend?'

'The one you spoke to here, the one who told you where I lived. She fancies you.'

I started to ask her for the address and then I noticed she had the same look in her eyes as when she'd talked about B.J.

'Not my type, sorry,' I said. That seemed to cheer her up a little bit and I left her there looking motherly. I made a mental note to call back and find the other one when I had time for such activities. What with the woman in the bar at the theatre, I was lining them up all over town. I might be headed for happier days. Once I'd managed to shake off all those who seemed intent on making my life miserable, if not actually dangerous.

I heard light footsteps behind me and Big Eric shuffled up in his black plimsolls. He bent an enquiring thumb at me.

'Surviving,' I answered. 'But only just.'

We went into the car-park and he had to help me climb up into the cab of the lorry.

He made a this-way, that-way gesture with his hands.

'I'm not sure,' I said. 'I think I'd better keep out of sight for a while. At least, overnight. I don't think I could run very fast at the moment.'

He grinned and jerked a thumbs-up at me and we rolled out of the car-park. With Big Eric standing up and occasionally jumping on and off the pedals we forged a way through the traffic until I could see we were heading towards his home.

I thought about arguing. I didn't want to involve him and Doris in my problems. Then I decided against arguing, partly because I knew he wouldn't listen and also because it crossed my mind that it wouldn't do any harm to try and interest his three sons in joining my team. I could do with the kind of protection they would be able to offer. Always assuming my powers of persuasion were up to the task.

I let my mind wander over what the nurse had told me and I realised I still had a problem of identification.

It didn't seem very likely that the men who had worked me over very successfully that afternoon would need to visit the Infirmary asking silly questions about Jenks. So, that meant the pudgy man, whoever he was, and B.J. were not mixed up with them. Which left me wondering who they were mixed up with. Probably one of them was with the fortune-teller's team but I hadn't the vaguest idea where the other one fitted in. Or which was which.

Was B.J. with the fortune-teller, or was she involved with someone else? Everything suddenly seemed more complicated than before.

I hadn't come up with any bright ideas when we reached North Road and I let Big Eric help me out of the cab and went in to spend a warm, comfortable, food-filled and carefree evening.

Well, almost carefree. I couldn't help thinking that unless I got some answers quickly I might find myself having to give back some of the property I had appropriated and that didn't seem at all like a good idea.

CHAPTER TEN

I slept on the floor of the unused front room on an improvised mattress made up of cushions from a three-piece suite. Although a considerable amount of heavy traffic used the road outside I slept better than I had for years, but I still woke up feeling as if one of the lorries had detoured across my body.

I staggered to my feet, switched on the light and peered at myself in the mirror over the fireplace. The left side of my face was swollen and was an interesting blend of red and blue but it was relatively pain free compared with the back of my head. I tentatively flexed my arms and legs and then tried some deep breathing.

That wasn't a very good idea and I started coughing which made matters even worse.

I was still trying to decide whether I should get dressed or simply lie down and die quietly when the door opened and Doris put her head around it smiling brightly at me.

'You're alive then?'

'Nearly,' I said.

She came into the room with a mug of tea and I took it from her gratefully.

'It came yesterday,' she said in a conspiratorial whisper.

That meant the money had arrived safely although I wasn't sure I'd gained anything now. I had pointed the finger at the Perkins' house by spending the night there.

'Thanks,' I said.

'Do you want it now?'

'No. Is it somewhere safe?'

'Yes. I haven't told the lads and I won't, but I don't like keeping secrets from Sid.'

'Keep it a secret just a little longer please, love,' I said. 'The fewer people who know about it the better, but if you feel you have to tell Big Eric then I don't mind.'

She nodded. 'I'll wait for a day or two then.' She hesitated. 'I saw Sandra's mother at the shops yesterday.'

'Oh yes.' I didn't ask how that old war horse was. Sandra's mother was one of those small, wiry, indestructible women who had grown up with a well developed sense of dislike for all things male and two husbands and three sons of her own hadn't done anything to make her change her mind by the time I came into her orbit. When I left her dislike had been sufficiently refuelled to keep her going with 'I-told-you-sos' for another thirty years.

'I asked her point blank about Sandra and whether or not she was getting married. She didn't want to answer at first but she looked sufficiently annoyed for it to be true.' I grinned, she would be annoyed too, her daughter going the same way as she'd gone herself. 'Anyway, she told me eventually. They're planning to marry as soon as he has a steady job.' That explained a lot. If lover-boy was on the dole then Sandra wouldn't be in too great a hurry to put the blight on my contribution towards her welfare, meagre though it was.

'I would've thought she'd had enough of layabouts,' I said. It was supposed to be a joke but Doris didn't take it as one.

'So would I,' she said. 'But she needs to have someone.'

'Needs?'

'She's pregnant.'

'Bloody hell.'

'Don't swear, Johnny,' she reproved me.

'Sorry. You have to admit though, it's a bit surprising.' It was to me. Sandra had never been backward in that particular area but at thirty-four she should have known better.

'Maybe you're right,' Doris said and sniffed her disapproval of the whole thing. 'Breakfast in ten minutes,' she added, dismissing the subject before disappearing through the doorway. I sat there, drinking the hot tea, trying to see if I cared about my ex-wife's pregnancy. I didn't, but I did feel a tinge of pity for lover-boy. He didn't know what he was letting himself in for.

I pulled my thoughts away to more important matters. It was becoming increasingly important that if I was to keep alive and well and able to spend the riches I hoped soon to call my own, I needed to keep well out of the clutches of the various groups who were gathering around me. All of them had different ideas about the distribution of my new-found wealth and I was beginning to think that simply going on the run would've been a better idea than trying to find out who really owned the diamonds and the money. I came to the conclusion there was still a hope that I could manage to keep them off my back with a minimum of aggravation.

The door opened again and Big Eric appeared, to collect my empty mug.

'Thanks,' I said. 'That helped.'

He grinned widely.

'Are the lads up yet?' I asked.

He shook his head.

'They're not working today?'

Another shake.

'Good. I'd like to talk to them before I go.'

He raised his eyebrows but didn't press the point.

Breakfasts at the Perkins' house are, by my standards, like lunch, dinner and supper all rolled into one. After I had waded through eggs and bacon, tomato and black pudding, fried bread and mushrooms I felt ready for another sleep but instead I went up into the bathroom and washed the parts of me that were not too painful or strapped up or unreachable without stretching something that didn't want to be stretched.

While I was in there I heard the three sons get up, each one trying the bathroom door before clattering noisily downstairs to start their weekend with what I knew would be breakfasts twice as big as the one I had just forced my way through.

From the bathroom I went down to the front room, tidied round and folded up the sheets and sleeping bag I had used and returned the cushions to the three-piece suite in the back room. Then I went into the kitchen and put my case to the Perkins' sons.

It didn't work. The three of them, all big men and all as hard as nails were not interested in me or my little problem. For Stan, at thirty-five the oldest, Saturdays were divided equally between the betting shop and Hull City if they were playing at home, which they were that day.

Joey, the middle one, spent his Saturdays commuting between the allotment, where he grew the massive vegetable supply his mother needed to feed them in the manner to which they'd become accustomed, and the Three Tuns where he helped the landlord maintain his reputation for selling a lot of beer. Sidney, the youngest, named after his father and always referred to, therefore, as Little Sidney, despite the fact that he was half as tall again as Big Eric, would spend his Saturday the way he spent all Saturdays, polishing and repolishing his motorbike. It was a fearsome, 1000 c.c. Honda that looked capable of almost anything and probably was.

The fact that I had materialised out of nowhere after a gap of six months and was asking them to protect me from a fate worse than death didn't cut a lot of ice. For a start I wouldn't, couldn't, tell them why I was in need of protection and they swiftly, and rightly, came to the conclusion that I was involved in something illegal. That was something they didn't want to know about. Added to that was the fact that, although they knew I liked their parents and that the feeling was reciprocated, we were no longer as friendly as we were as children. That was chiefly because they were always engaged in pursuits that didn't appeal to me and I'd had my own friends, the layabouts with whom I went thieving. That put a gulf between us the passage of years had merely widened.

I sat there, accepting the fact that, like it or not, and I didn't like it, I was on my own.

Eventually Big Eric tapped me on the shoulder and indicated that, even if his sons planned to spend the day idling around their home, he had work to do and was leaving for the fairground. I let him drive me back to Park Street so that I could collect my car.

After the bright red lorry had driven off, painted lions and elephants and all, I went up to my room and checked that nobody had torn up any more floorboards. then I went down and rapped loudly on Carole's door. Eventually she let me in and delivered a few obscure obscenties from which I gathered she hadn't got to bed until after five.

'I can't help it if you've got into bad ways,' I told her.

'Oh, Jesus Christ,' she said and fell back onto the bed, the wrap-over robe she was wearing falling open in a way that began to give me ideas, despite the slightly shattered state I was in. Then I realised she was crying and I sat down on the bed beside her, reluctantly pulled a sheet over her and put my arms around her until the tears subsided.

'Are you going to tell me what all that was about?' I asked.

'Everything,' she said.

'You'll have to explain.'

She pulled away slightly but I held onto her. 'There's nothing you can do,' she said.

'Try me.'

'You know what I'm like, Johnny. Drink, men.'

'The drinking is something you can overcome if you try hard enough,' I said, aware that I sounded uncharacteristically pious.

'Not as long as it helps me forget the way I am about men.'

'Even that's something you can overcome,' I said, for something to say.

'Christ, don't talk like a fool,' she snapped at me. 'Do you think I *like* being the way I am about men? Have you any idea what it's like? It isn't just wanting it, the way you want it. It's needing it, needing it like a drug, like ... like the way I need a drink. I have to have sex whether I like it or not and that means I can't always make a free choice when it comes to who I have it with.'

I couldn't think of anything to say that wouldn't sound as foolishly inept as my earlier remark, so when she stopped talking I said nothing. Instead I sat there, my arms still around her, trying to determine just what my feelings were towards her. Despite the way I felt the last time we slept together I knew that I felt more affection for her than for any of the other women into whose lives I had drifted, only to drift out again before anything stuck, since Sandra and I had parted.

I was coming to the unsatisfactory and not very pleasing conclusion that even with her twin problems of men and drink, Carole Dixon was a lot closer to my kind of woman than I wanted to admit. Which made me determined to try to decide just what was my kind of woman.

My ex-wife wasn't my kind of woman, and presumably, B.J. Williams wasn't, so who was? Fireside, pipe and slippers wasn't for me. Children weren't either, that was obvious from the casual way I'd let Sandra take Susie out of my life and indoctrinate her into thinking I was in league with the Devil. So maybe the easy-going, pleasure-seeking type, like Carole, really was my type. Then I corrected myself, easy-going, pleasure-seeking type Carole had been. That she was now something very different was, perhaps, a warning of the way I'd end up myself if I continued drifting as I had done during the past few years.

I came to the conclusion that I wasn't coming to any conclusions. All I was doing was confusing the issue and myself into the bargain. One thing was certain, however. I would have to ensure I didn't unnecessarily complicate my life, any part of it and certainly not the sexual part, before those few thousand pounds were safe and soundly where the opposition couldn't get them. More to the point, where the opposition wouldn't even begin to suspect they were. That would be time enough to sort out my private life.

Carole moved slightly and it occurred to me that a suitable type for me would be a non-drinking, non-man hungry version of Carole. She moved again and this time pulled right away and I let her go. She stood up, walked across the room and pulled back the curtain to the alcove. I watched her as she filled the kettle and switched it on. As she turned back towards me the still unfastened robe swung open and I saw heavy bruises that hadn't been there when we had been together a couple of nights before.

'What happened?' I asked, pointing.

She looked down, totally unembarassed at her near nakedness. 'What I was telling you about,' she said. 'When you're the way I am, choice is something that isn't often permitted. You have to take what you can get, lumps and all.'

I felt helpless and sounded it. 'Is there anything I can do?'

'Like marry me and carry me off to a better land where all is sunshine and light and where I can be expensively dried-out for evermore?' There was a mixture of bitterness and regret in her voice and I recalled, with a mild feeling of guilt, my thoughts of a moment or two earlier.

'Marrying you wouldn't do either of us any good,' I said, honestly. 'As for sunshine and light, well, a couple of weeks in Spain might be possible if I can pull off a deal I'm working on.'

'And the drying out?'

'That's something you'll have to do for yourself,' I said.

She smiled at that, something approaching her normal smile. 'Don't I know it.'

The kettle boiled and she made two cups of instant coffee and handed one to me before crawling back into bed. She sipped at her cup for a few moments and then, casually, asked if I had meant it when I had offered a holiday in the sun.

'Why not?'

'What is the deal you're working on, or shouldn't I ask?'

'The less you know the better.'

'I can be trusted.'

'Of course you can. It's just that. . . .' I hesitated. 'Well, someone offered me a job. Then he died suddenly before he could set it up. Now I hope to carry on without him.'

'The man who died, did he die naturally? I mean there was nothing. . . .'

'No, nobody killed him. He had a heart attack.'

'Who was he?'

'His name was Jenks, Claude Jenks. At least that's the name he was using. He was quite something to look at. Covered in tattooes, a mass of them. He had some connection with the circus. A friend of mine knew of him, but under a different name.'

'What name?'

'I don't know, I didn't ask. It's difficult talking to Big Eric.'

'Who?'

I told her about Big Eric.

'He's in town for the Fair?'

'Yes.'

'Then he'll be away again?'

'Yes.' I hadn't wanted to talk about Big Eric but it seemed safer ground. Certainly Carole seemed to have recovered from her earlier depression.

'Where are you going now?' she asked me.

'Just one or two little calls to make.'

'You . . . you can stop here for a while if you want to.'

'No, I. . . .'

She stopped me by touching her finger to my lips. 'I'm not asking you to fill a need. Just if you want to that's all.'

'Thanks,' I said. 'It's the best offer I've had for a long time. Promise you won't cross me off your list if I refuse.'

She smiled and shook her head. I leaned over and kissed her then stood up and took my empty coffee cup into the alcove. On the way back I glanced at the pile of records and cassettes and the stereo equipment I'd piled up there.

'Do you want that lot out of your way?' I asked.

'It's not in the way.'

'I can set it up if you want to play anything.'

'No, don't bother. I've heard the things you play. I prefer dreamy ones that make no demands.'

I nodded in agreement, I knew what she meant. There were enough demands being made upon her without becoming deeply involved in anything she didn't have to.

I left her looking slightly more relaxed than she had been when I had arrived, which wasn't the effect I'd been having on people recently. It gave me an unwarranted feeling of well-being that lasted all the way across town to the office Inspector Gostelow nearly filled with his huge, bear-like, bulk.

'Been getting yourself into bother again, I see,' he said, nodding his head at my technicoloured face.

'Nothing that your lads weren't supposed to prevent,' I said, righteously.

He leaned over the desk and seemed to swell to twice his already considerable size. 'What gives you the idea my men are employed for the express purpose of protecting toe-rags like you,' he said.

'Cut out the insults, Gostelow,' I said.

'Inspector Gostelow, to you.'

'You can still cut them out. I haven't committed any crime. It was your idea to send two men out to protect me. . . .'

'Protect you,' he interrupted. 'Listen to me, Baxter, I am not interested in whether or not you get thumped every day for a month. If someone thinks it's worth risking their knuckles on you then the chances are you're up to no good and you probably deserve every punch.'

'And kick?' I asked.

'And kick,' he agreed.

'What took me off your list of favourite people?'

'You were never on it.'

I took a deep breath and decided pacification was in order. 'Look, I don't know what I've done to deserve all this, but what's changed since I was in here last time?'

'You've had a beating, no, two beatings. According to my lads, the one they interrupted wasn't all that bad, but last night's was an ambulance and hospital job. That's what's changed things.'

'They've changed things for me, but why you?'

'Because if somebody doesn't like you enough to work you over then, as I've said, you must have done something to deserve it. What's more, the odds are the something was illegal.'

'So why were your lads watching me, if it wasn't to save my skin?'

'Save your skin? You must be joking, lad. They have better things to do with their time than save you from a thumping I have no doubt you deserved.'

'Then why were they there?'

'That's for me to know and for you to find out,' he said, obscurely.

'So where do we go from here?'

'Why are you here?'

'To make sure I don't get another thumping.'

'Do you think I care?'

'Don't you?'

'Don't ask silly questions. I couldn't care less if they kick your brains out next time. Always assuming you have any up there.'

We weren't getting anywhere and I could see my chances of ensuring I had a protective shield around me when I went back to the fairground that afternoon for my meeting with the fortune-teller, were diminishing with every insult.

I decided to try once more for pacification. 'Alright, I give in, what do you want?'

He hunched forward in his seat once again. 'Claude Jenks.'

'What about him?'

'Tell me everything you know about him.'

'I already have.'

He stood up. 'On your way,' he said.

'Alright, I asked a few questions, I know that he was connected with the circus.'

'I would've thought that was obvious.'

'It was, but I confirmed it.'

'How?'

I didn't want to involve Big Eric. 'I know a

few people in that line and I just asked around.'

'Is that why you were at the fairground?'

'Yes.'

'Why have you suddenly become a target?'

'I don't know.' His face changed so I went on, 'From what the heavies said who did the beating, they're looking for something Jenks had when he died.'

'And they think you've got it?'

'It seems so.'

'Have you?'

'I wasn't with him when he died,' I said. 'According to what I've been told, you're the one who took away his personal effects.'

His colour darkened. 'Meaning?'

'Meaning that if there was nothing there when he died they must be mistaken.'

He cooled off a little. 'You're sure he didn't give you anything?'

'Positive.'

He looked at me for a long time but in the end he believed me. There was no reason why he shouldn't, that part was perfectly true.

'Okay,' he said. 'I'll keep up surveillance on you for a few days more.'

'Thank you,' I said, politely.

He grinned suddenly. 'Some kind of a record for a man like you, isn't it? Asking for police protection.'

'What kind of man do you think I am?'

'One I wouldn't trust with either my wallet or

my daughter,' he said. He opened the door and I stood up and went out into the corridor and let him lead me to the exit.

'Where are you going now?' he asked.

'To the fair,' I said.

'Pushing your luck, aren't you?'

'I fancy some candyfloss and a ride on the Dodgems.'

'I'll bet,' he said, just to prove he was smarter than I was.

'I'm parked around the corner in Dock Street,' I said.

'Give my lad five minutes.'

'Right.' I left him there, walked to the Cortina and spent the five minutes thinking about Inspector Gostelow. I couldn't make up my mind how much he knew. Certainly he knew a lot more than he'd let on to me but I was reasonably certain he didn't know what Jenks had been carrying. I was absolutely certain he didn't know I now had it and although he might suspect I knew more than I'd admitted he wasn't sure. For the moment it didn't matter, what mattered was that I'd got what I wanted. Protection against another beating. At least I hoped I had, although, when a small unmarked Minivan peeped its horn as it drove slowly past, I wasn't too sure. From somewhere Gostelow had unearthed another fourteen year old copper.

I started the engine and drove off, letting my guardian angel fall into convoy behind me.

I pushed a cassette into the deck and let Carl Fontana's version of *A Beautiful Friendship* wash over me. Listening to his trombone playing reminded me of the young trombone-player I'd heard at the Humberside Theatre's jam session, a connection that would have made the young man's day if he'd known I put him into the same thought as someone of Fontana's class. Then my mind registered the conversations I'd had at the bar that same lunchtime and I suddenly realised I wasn't as smart as I thought I was.

CHAPTER ELEVEN

Although the fairground wouldn't really swing until after dark, when the lights and noise would turn it into another world, there were still a few thousand people jammed into the spaces between the stalls and rides. Mostly youngsters, older people would be there later re-living their own youth.

I wandered about, apparently aimlessly but all the time ensuring that I saw and registered as many of the adult faces I could. I also made sure my young policeman friend didn't lose me although I noticed that he didn't join me when I tried out a few of the less violent rides. I decided against things like the Whip on the grounds that it might undo some of the good done by the bandages put on at the Infirmary.

Five o'clock came eventually and I walked across to the fortune-teller's caravan and joined a small queue of giggling young girls waiting to be told whether to look out for tall dark or short fair men. I watched them incuriously for a moment and then it suddenly occurred to me they were about the same age as Susie. Quite unexpectedly I felt a twinge at the thought that if Sandra did remarry I would see even less of Susie than I had in the past. I wasn't sure what the emotion was that I was feeling but it was disturbing enough to make me try to force my mind to other things. It didn't prove a very easy task.

When it was my turn I went up the steps, glancing round to see where the policeman was. He was rolling coins at a near-by stall and carefully avoiding my eye.

The fortune-teller didn't look as I came in and dropped into the seat opposite her. 'Are you going to tell my fortune or shall I tell yours?' I asked.

She looked up at me and started to speak, then realised that I didn't look the way I had looked the previous afternoon.

'The opposition,' I said, in reply to her unasked question.

'Oh?'

'Seems they object to me having their

property.'

'Who were they?'

'Friends of the tatooed man.'

'Did you hand them over?'

'What do you think?'

'Do you know what you're involved in?' she asked.

'No, and before you tell me, I don't want to know.'

'Afraid I'll frighten you off?'

'If you like. Right, you want the consignment, I know where it is. How much?'

'We think you should state the price.'

'Do you?'

'Yes.'

'You and your friend.'

'Yes.'

I looked at her thoughtfully and then grinned. 'I'm not sure he's all that smart.'

'Oh?' I had her puzzled.

'He talks too much.'

'Does he?' Now she was slightly worried.

'Yes. We were talking in the bar at the Humberside Theatre and he let something slip.'

Now she was definitely worried. 'Did he?'

'He said something about Jenks being tattooed all over, something he couldn't have known from seeing him at the Haworth Arms last Tuesday night.'

She frowned at that. 'He ... he said that did he?'

147

'Yes. And another thing, he's a bloody awful cornet-player.'

She smiled. 'I wouldn't know about that,' she said. 'I'm tone deaf.' She leaned back in her seat and smiled again. I had a sudden, uneasy feeling that I'd gone wrong somewhere. She was no longer worried.

'So, you want me to name a price,' I said, pulling the discussion back to where I really wanted it.

'Yes.'

'Okay. Forty thousand pounds.' There was a long silence. I don't know where the figure came from but it had a nice rounded sound to it. Then the silence broke as she started to laugh.

I let her go on for a few moments. 'Alright,' I said, 'so I'm a comic.'

'I should say you are,' she said. 'Five thousand.'

I shook my head and stood up. 'Sorry, you'd better get on with your fortune-telling. That's much more your style.'

'Sit down, Mr. Baxter,' she said. Her voice showed a little steel and I sat down and waited. 'Alright. Cards on the table.'

'Can't think of a better place for it,' I said.

She scowled at my flippancy. 'You're not a big-time criminal,' she said.

'Get on with it,' I said. 'Forget the character analysis and get on with the business.'

'There isn't anywhere you can take the

stones. Nowhere at all. If you try it, you'll have the police on your back in no seconds flat.'

'So?'

'The other side won't pay you anything. All they'll do, if you push them, is write off the consignment and write you off with it.'

'Well?'

'That leaves us. We're the only ones you can trust.'

'Christ...'

'Please do not blaspheme in here,' she said coldly. 'This is my home.'

She meant it too. 'Alright, let's say I trust you.'

'Ten thousand.'

'Thirty.'

'Fifteen and that's...'

'Never say it's your last offer if it isn't. I might just believe you.'

She glared at me and then nodded her head. 'Your move,' she said.

'Twenty-five and a guarantee,' I said.

'What kind of guarantee?'

'I want the other side to know you've got the consignment.'

'We're not fools.'

'And neither am I. As long as they think I've got the package they'll keep after me.'

She thought about that. 'I suppose you're right but that isn't our problem is it?'

'I'm making it your problem.'

'Alright. I'll see to it they know, although I can't promise they won't deal with you anyway.'

'I'll take care they don't get the chance until they've had time to cool off. Okay, we have a deal, twenty-five thousand and the guarantee.'

'You're a jump ahead. I've agreed to the guarantee but not the price.'

'Now, listen . . .'

'Twenty thousand. Take it or leave it. And that *is* my final offer.'

I looked at her in silence, wondering just what the real value of the stones was. If the fortune-teller was prepared to give me twenty thousand pounds they must be worth five times that. At least. The future looked suddenly brighter.

'A deal,' I said. I stood up again and held out a hand in what I hoped was the approved manner for concluding a transaction of that nature. The fortune-teller looked at my outstretched palm as if I was out of my mind.

'What do you want? Your fortune telling?'

I pulled my hand away. 'No thanks. I make my own future.'

She looked at me with a gleam of cynicism in her dark eyes. 'So do we,' she said.

I left her sitting there and went out of the caravan and past the queue that had grown a lot longer during the time I had been there. I wondered whether there had been any hidden message in her last remark. There didn't seem to be.

I walked across to the coin-rolling stall.

'Winning?' I asked the young policeman.

'Does anyone?' he said, glumly.

I felt like telling him some of us did, but I knew everything that had happened so far would be reported back to Gostelow. All but the conversation inside the caravan. He wouldn't know about that and that was all that mattered.

'Had enough?' I asked him.

He jingled the small change in his pocket and nodded his head. 'Where now?'

'Just drive around the town to see what we pick up.'

He looked at me curiously but he'd had his orders and he wasn't going to risk incurring the wrath of Inspector Gostelow.

'Right,' he said.

We had been obliged to park some distance away from the fairground as on-street parking was drastically restricted in the area during that week.

The ritual Fair-week drizzle of rain had begun whilst I was in the caravan and I was thankful that I'd spent some of my ill-gotten gains on waterproofing myself.

Halfway to the car I saw a BBC van and stopped out of curiosity. It was from the local radio station and standing on the pavement, talking animatedly, were B.J. Williams and Phillip Jason. Jason was still wearing a now-damp corduroy jacket and sandals but he had exchanged his pink shirt for a lime-green one.

'Hello, girls.' I said.

'Oh, hello, dear,' Jason said. B.J. glared at me without acknowledging my greeting.

'What brings you here?'

'Just a little thing we're doing for our arts programme,' B.J. said.

'What's artistic about that lot,' I said, waving an arm at the fairground, already beginning to gleam brightly as the sky darkened.

'Everything, if you have a soul,' Jason said.

He sounded as if he meant it. I looked at B.J. 'A word,' I said and stepped away.

Reluctantly she followed me. 'What do you want?'

'To talk.'

'Then talk.'

'Not here.'

'What about?'

'Something important.'

She glared at me, then, seeing I was serious thought for a moment. 'I'll be here for a couple of hours then I have to go back to the studio. Pick me up there at eight-thirty.' She turned away before I could agree or argue so I fluttered my fingers at Jason who smiled happily at me and I left them to their artistic endeavours.

I drove into the city centre, parked outside the public library and went inside and up to the first floor. I looked behind the shelf of American telephone directories for Wichita and

Wilmington. The package had gone, so the two men who had shown me they knew a thing or two about physical violence would be well and truly steaming by now.

I returned to the car with my young watcher close behind me. I stopped and let him catch up with me.

'Fancy a drink?' I asked.

'I'm on duty.'

'Since when did that stop a policeman from drinking?'

'Who's paying?'

'I will,' I said, generously.

'Come into money, have you,' he said, looking interested.

'Leave the detective work to Big Chief Grizzly Bear,' I said.

'Inspector Gostelow is a respected officer,' he said firmly.

'Or, putting it another way, you're all scared to death of him.'

'You might be right,' he said. 'What about that drink.'

We went into the Oasis, a basement wine-bar that was unexpectedly located and equally unexpectedly comfortable and pleasant. There was also piped music which I can usually do without but which, on this occasion, was acceptable. In England, you don't often drink to the music of the Swing Era. Not really my scene but a big improvement on the usual pre-digested

153

pop you hear.

I drank scotch and the young policeman settled for a glass of red wine. We sat and talked about motor cars and football, two topics about which I know very little and like even less.

Eventually it was time to go and collect B.J. and I led the way back up the steps to pavement level. I told him where I was going and where I expected to go next, just in case he lost me. I didn't want him out of the way just yet.

It was exactly eight-thirty when I drew up outside the BBC studio in Chapel Street. As I stopped the door opened and B.J. walked out. That could have been because she was a naturally good timekeeper or because she had been watching for me. I had a depressing feeling it was more likely to be the former.

'What do you want to see me about?' she asked, almost before I'd moved off.

'To talk.'

'What about?'

'How about mutual friends?'

'Be serious.'

'Alright, how about riches beyond the dreams of avarice. Or is that too artistic for you?'

She didn't answer for some moments, by which time I had negotiated the one-way system and was heading north on Beverley Road.

'I take it you have something to say that you think is valuable and important enough for all this cloak-and-dagger nonsense.'

'I think so,' I touched my face. 'And I'm not the only one.'

She looked at me closely for the first time and even in the shifting light from street lamps she could see enough to know I'd been in trouble.

'Who did that?'

'Maybe it was one of the mutual friends I mentioned.'

'With friends like that. . . .'

'. . . who needs enemies,' we finished together.

There was silence again but it was less glacial than before.

'What happened?' she said eventually, her voice softening a little.

'Wait, we're nearly there.'

'Where are we going?'

I slowed to turn into the entrance to Pearson Park. 'Where do you think?' I said.

'I don't remember inviting you home,' she said.

'Maybe not but I remember my last visit with a warm glow.'

'Nothing happened that needs repetition,' she said, a slight coolness returning.

'Didn't it?' I said. I stopped outside the house where she had her flat and turned off the ignition.

Neither of us spoke and then, with something that sounded suspiciously like a sigh, she opened the door and climbed out. I locked the car and

155

followed her, after glancing down the road that skirted the park to ensure the Minivan was strategically placed where the driver could hear my screams for help if things got beyond me.

I had every hope they would not.

CHAPTER TWELVE

My hopes of not needing his help were fulfilled, but not in the way I expected. Things very rapidly showed themselves to be running on different lines to my last visit. No offer of a drink, no offer of a shower to cleanse away the grime that seemed to have offended her and the bedroom door remained obstinately closed.

When it became obvious that I wouldn't have to scream for help I decided it would be best to get down to business and then out of there before my ego suffered irreparable damage.

'Bristol,' I said.

She frowned, but there was something there. Something that could have been alarm. 'What about Bristol?'

'You were there a few weeks ago?'

'So?'

'So were a lot of other interesting people.'

'Make sense,' she snapped.

'What happened to the warm friendliness of . . .'

'Keep to the point.'

I shrugged. 'Alright. What were you doing in Bristol?'

'What has that to do with you?'

I turned towards the door. 'Okay, suit yourself.'

She let me get to the door and turn the handle before she spoke. 'I was there on an exchange with their local radio station.'

'So I heard,' I said, without turning.

'Then why ask?'

This time I turned round and looked at her carefully. Her face was flushed and angry. I had an image of her, stretching her naked body across the bed only two days earlier. It seemed like a thousand years ago. Then I pushed away the thought, it was obvious that whatever had precipitated that particular sexual encounter, it wasn't about to be repeated.

'What else did you do there, who else did you meet?'

She opened her mouth to answer sharply and then stopped. Her white teeth bit down on her lower lip for a few seconds.

'Why do you think it's important to you?' she said eventually.

'Some people who are here, in Hull, were also in Bristol a few weeks ago. Not just you, but several others.'

'So?'

'I seem to be mixed up in their affairs.'

157

'Oh?'

'With reason.'

'Oh?' she said again but this time she was interested.

'I have something they want.'

'What?'

'Can't you guess.'

'How could I?'

I grinned at her. 'If you can't guess then maybe I'm wasting my time.'

'Alright, what do you want?'

'I want to do a deal.'

'What kind of deal?'

'One where somebody gives me a lot of money.'

'In return for what?'

'For the things we were talking about.'

'Which are?'

I sighed theatrically. 'Now we're back where we started.'

She looked at me in silence for several long moments. 'Wait here,' she said. She went across to the bedroom door, opened it and went in, closing it behind her. After a moment I heard music. She had switched on her stereo, which seemed an odd thing to do at that particular moment, so I went close to the door and listened. I heard a faint tinkling that didn't seem to be part of the music. She was making a telephone call and after a moment I heard her speak but I couldn't make out the words.

Then I heard the bell tinkle again and I moved smartly back across the room. She didn't come out immediately, and I began to wonder if she was making another call. Then the door opened and she came out. We had both been standing, arguing, in the clothes we were wearing when we came into the flat, her hospitality not having been very much in evidence. Now, she had taken off her outdoor coat and, although I couldn't be certain, I think she had changed her dress. The one she wore didn't look like the kind of thing she would have been wearing, even under a coat, at either the studio or for a meeting with Jason at the fairground. She had left the bedroom door open too and she hadn't turned off the music. It was Johnny Mathis again and my earlier assumption that the evening wouldn't be a repetition began to fade as pleasurable anticipation took over.

'A drink?' she asked.

'Please.'

'Scotch, isn't it?'

'Yes.'

She poured out two drinks and then sat down, confirming I'd been right about the dress. It fell away displaying a considerable length of her long legs. Definitely not the thing to wear for a tramp round a fairground.

'So, where were we,' I said, when she had arranged herself.

She smiled at me for the first time. 'Do we

have to talk about it now, can't it wait?'

'I expect so,' I said. I stood the glass of whisky on a table and slipped off my anorak. The movement hurt and it must have shown on my face because she stood up and came over to me.

'Are you alright?' she asked, seemingly concerned.

'I've felt better.'

'We'd better be a little more gentle than we were last time,' she said.

I let her draw me towards the bedroom door but my mind was no longer anticipating the possibilities of further gymnastics. The change was too sudden and the similarity between what was happening and what had happened on the last occasion was too obvious to miss. The soft lights and sweet music and the sudden, almost nymphomaniacal, interest in my body. From the way Carole behaved I knew enough to know that, whatever B.J. was up to, it wasn't precipitated by some inner compulsion.

It had to be the telephone call, just as there had been a telephone call the last time. A telephone call first and then a single unanswered ring later, to tell her that whatever was being done whilst I was otherwise engaged had been completed.

I let her lead me into the bedroom but my eyes and thoughts were not on the deliberately provocative movements of her body. I took in a

160

couple of things fairly rapidly. One was that the telephone was plugged into a jack-point and the other was that the bedroom door had a lock on it and there was a key on the inside.

I let her help me remove my leather jacket but I took care to drop it on a chair by the door. She lay back on the bed and I leaned over her and kissed her, letting my hands run over the soft material of her dress. She was wearing nothing beneath it and I had a momentary thought that it would be nice to set aside my suspicions and take advantage of what was being offered, because there seemed little doubt that, after this, there would be no more offers. I reached behind her, found the zip fastener of the dress and drew it down. It went a long way, well below her waist. Then I pulled her dress forward and down until it was wrapped around her beautiful legs. I kissed her neatly on each breast and then, for old times sake, where her thighs came together in a warm dark tangle.

Then, I reached for the light switch and as the room darkened, yanked out the telephone jack and headed for the door. I had the key out of the lock and, to save time had heaved the telephone into the middle of the sitting-room, before B.J. realised what was happening.

'What . . .'

I looked back into the bedroom. She was struggling awkwardly, the dress twisting around her legs as she tried to scramble off the bed.

Regretfully, I took my coat off the chair by the door and locked her in.

I put my jacket on and struggled into my anorak. Inside the bedroom I heard her try the door once and then nothing. I wasn't surprised, banging hysterically on the door wasn't her style.

I went over to the door and tapped gently. 'B.J., can you hear me?'

Silence.

'Sorry,' I said. I meant it, I was sorry. 'Go to bed, I'll see that you're released by morning.'

Silence.

'Bye B.J.,' I said.

'You're making a mistake,' she said, her voice distant but clear.

'I'm an expert at that,' I told her.

'You're in something that's too big for you.'

'So people keep telling me.'

I picked up the telephone and, just in case, took it into the kitchen and dropped it into a pedal-bin. Then I went out of the flat and down to the Cortina, not running but not wasting any time either.

I wasn't sure what her performance had been about but the last time she had distracted me someone had ripped my room apart. They hadn't found anything and it didn't seem likely they would look there again. That left a couple of possibilities and I didn't much like the thought of either of them.

It also told me something else I couldn't quite fit in. It didn't seem very likely the fortune-teller and her friends were behind this particular operation. As far as they were concerned they believed I was a mug and had every intention of doing a deal with them. Neither could I see the two men who had beten me up in the circus tent playing the kind of delicate game B.J. had tried. When they caught up with me they wouldn't bother with any finesse, they'd just kick the truth out of me.

So whoever B.J. was tied up with, it didn't seem to be any of the other parties interested in the whereabouts of the tattooed man's diamonds. Life wasn't getting any less complicated.

For no better reason than it was closest, I went back to Park Street. If my guess was right, there were two possible places B.J.'s friend would be looking and Carole's room was one of them. I parked the Cortina some distance away and waited until the Minivan with the young policeman had pulled in behind me.

'I think there might be a little bit of bother,' I told him. 'Don't come up with me but don't stay far away in case things happen.'

'Such as?' He sounded quite eager, I suppose he must've been getting bored.

'I don't know, but keep your eyes open and come up if I start screaming.'

I left him and went up the stairs, silently,

feeling anything but heroic. At Carole's door I stopped and listened. At first I didn't hear anything but then I heard a sound, as if someone was gasping for breath. The sound didn't get louder as I listened, it was almost rhythmic and I began to wonder if I'd guessed wrong. It sounded as if Carole was entertaining.

I went on up the stairs to my room to see if I'd had visitors. I hadn't. I stood for a moment, uncertain. Then I heard the door on the lower landing open and close. I flicked out my light, opened the door and moved softly onto the landing. The figure of a man was outside Carole's door and as I watched another came out of her room and joined him. It was too dark to identify them but, instinctively, I knew they hadn't been in her room for the reasons I'd first thought. I started down towards them but they turned and clattered down the stairs.

I yelled out, regretting that I hadn't bothered to ask the young policeman for his name. I went down the stairs in a rush and into Carole's room. The place was a mess. Furniture was lying all over the room, some of it broken, and the contents of drawers were scattered everywhere. There was a mound of crumpled sheets and blankets on the bed and from them I could hear the faint, rhythmic sound I'd heard before, only this time it was clear, it was a woman sobbing. Not just crying but a deep-seated, wrenching sound. I pulled back the sheets.

164

She was lying face downwards, completely naked, and I gently turned her over, aware that as my hands touched her, her entire body jerked as if stung. Her face was a mass of contusions, whoever had beaten her made what happened to me look like the work of an amateur. A fine trickle of blood ran from one nostril and another from the corner of her mouth.

I heard footsteps on the stairs and the young policeman came into the room.

'Sorry,' he said. 'They ran for it, in different directions. I tried chasing one of...' He saw Carole and stopped. 'Good God. Did they...?'

'Yes,' I said tightly.

'I'll call in for an ambulance.'

'There's a 'phone on the landing.'

Carole opened her eyes and saw it was me. 'Johnny...' she said.

'Don't talk, we'll soon have you in hosptial.'

'I'm sorry...'

'What have you to be sorry about?'

'I...'

'I said, don't talk.'

I looked around the room. They had done a pretty good job of it. My record player was smashed into matchwood and someone had stamped all over my cassettes and records. I saw Carole move her head to follow my eyes.

'I'm sorry,' she said again.

'Worse things happen at sea.'

The young policeman stuck his head around

165

the door. 'Two minutes,' he said.

'Right.' I stood up and searched through the clothes on the floor until I found the wrap-over robe Carole had been wearing the last time I had been there. Awkwardly, I managed to get it on her and by the time I had done so the ambulance arrived.

'I'll follow you,' I said, as the ambulance men began the tricky task of negotiating the stairs.

'I'll wait here,' the policeman said.

I looked at him and nodded. Then I took another look at the room.

'Is this what you were expecting?' he said.

'No.'

'You were expecting something?'

I nodded. My mind was elsewhere. What had happened there had taken too long for it to have been set up by B.J. Williams' telephone call. I shook my head slowly. If she hadn't been setting this up then perhaps my second choice was the right one. Just then the telephone rang.

'I'll get it.' The policeman was out of the door before I could move.

I took advantage of his absence and crossed quickly to the pile of cassettes that had been thrown into a heap in the corner and apparently trampled on. It took me a few seconds to find the one I was looking for and I had just slipped it into my pocket when the policeman came back.

'Who was it?'

'Nobody. Just a tapping on the line. Kids I expect.'

'I'll...' The telephone rang again, interrupting me. 'I'll get it,' I finished. I picked up the receiver and gave my name. There was a tapping sound, as if someone was flicking a fingernail against the mouthpiece. 'Who is it?' I snapped.

More tapping.

'Look, stop playing games or I'll call the police,' I said.

The tapping came again, somehow urgent. My second choice for where B.J.'s telephone colleagues had been heading was in the back of my mind and suddenly the tapping sound made sense.

'Big Eric, is that you?'

More tapping.

'Look, if it is, tap twice.'

Two taps.

'Where are you? At the fair? Look, tap twice for yes, tap once for no.'

Christ, I thought, I sound like a bloody medium at a seance.

There was one tap.

'At home?'

Two taps.

'Trouble?'

Two taps.

'The lads, are they there?'

One tap.

'I'm on my way. Ten minutes. Okay?'

Two taps and then the telephone was replaced. I turned round to see the policeman looking at me as if I was out of my mind.

'What was all that about?'

'My nightly communing with the spirit world,' I said. I started for the stairs.

'Mr. Gostelow is on his way here,' he announced. 'You'd better wait.'

'Mr. Gostelow can...' There was no point in antagonising people for the sake of it. 'Tell him I can't wait around for him while all my friends get their heads beaten in.' I left him and went on down the stairs and into the Cortina. I wasn't in a very happy state of mind. I was being outguessed all along the line and that wouldn't do. It wouldn't do at all. Certainly not if I expected to wrap up a nice little deal for myself within the next few hours. Then I thought about the urgent sound Big Eric had made on the telephone and remembering Carole's battered face I felt a momentary twinge of conscience. As I'd said to the young policeman, all around me my friends were getting into trouble not of their own choosing. And it was my fault, and all I could do was worry about the money I planned to make.

For the first time in years I began to think about other people before myself. It was an unusual state of mind for me to be in and I wasn't sure I liked it. On the other hand I didn't actually dislike it either.

After I'd finished congratulating myself, cautiously, on my new-found state of moral uplift I thought about B.J. Williams. All my earlier daydreaming about her seemed to have faded into nothingness. It wasn't a result of any particularly startling revelations, just a realisation that, apart from being on the side of those dedicated to getting between me and what I was already thinking of as *my* diamonds, she was also unattainable. Even if circumstances had been different she would still have been out of my reach. She was glossy magazine material and I was much closer to gutter press. I shook my head in mild irritation. What with that kind of thinking and the fact that I was starting to think about other people first, I was acting like someone who, after a lifetime of sin, had suddenly found religion.

Hallelujah Baxter. I felt a grin come onto my face but then I thought again about Big Eric's urgent tapping and the grin faded as I pressed down on the accelerator. There would be time for self-congratulations later, when I had made certain that the few people I really liked in this world were not in trouble. Trouble brought to their door by nothing more damaging than the fact that they knew me. And that I had used them.

CHAPTER THIRTEEN

It took me more than the ten minutes I'd expected because I'd overlooked the traffic problems the Fair created on the two main roads that were my fastest routes to North Road. I had to make a detour down onto Hessle Road and then back up again and by the time I reached the Perkins' house in North Road more than twenty minutes had elapsed since Big Eric's phone call.

He was waiting for me when I opened the front door and walked straight in. He led me into the small, cosy living-room at the back of the house and it was like my room and Carole's all over again. The place was in a state of upheaval that turned it from what it had been into another world. My kind of world, and the unpleasant feeling I'd experienced in the car came back, stronger than ever. I was being forced to accept that I hadn't any right to inflict this kind of thing on people like the Perkins'.

'Where's Aunt Doris?' I asked Big Eric.

He pointed upwards and I let him lead me up the stairs. It was the first time I'd seen Doris Perkins anywhere but in her kitchen and she looked totally different. She was lying on the bed and she seemed to have shrunk in size and the bright red of her cheeks had dulled.

'I'm sorry,' I said.

'It wasn't your fault,' she said.

'Did they hurt you?'

'No, they didn't touch me. One of them held me while the other searched the house.'

I looked round the bedroom. It was in the same state as the room below.

'Everywhere?' I asked.

She nodded. 'Everywhere.'

There was a sound from below and I turned to see Big Eric leave the room and head down the stairs. I recognised the voices of two of their sons and I relaxed but only for the split-second it took me to realise that, when they saw what had happened, I would be in for a hard time if they associated it with me.

Doris read my thoughts. 'I won't tell them what they were looking for,' she said quietly.

'Thanks. Er, did . . .'

'No, I didn't tell them where it was. I think they thought you'd hidden it here without my knowledge.'

'Where . . .' I didn't get the question out because footsteps thundered up the stairs and Joey and Little Sidney loomed into the room. Their faces reflected only a fleeting recognition of me and then they turned to their mother. I slid out of the room and down the stairs and began to help Big Eric tidy things up, although all my instincts yelled out that I should get away before the lads came downstairs.

'I'm sorry,' I said to the little man. 'It's my

fault.'

He shook his head and held a finger to his lips.

I nodded and carried on, trying to bring some sort of order to the room.

Little Sidney was the first to come down the stairs and he stood in the doorway watching us. I did my best to avoid his eyes.

'Is this something to do with you?' he said eventually.

I took a deep breath, glanced at Big Eric and then nodded my head. 'I think so,' I told him.

He took a step into the room. 'Explain,' he said.

'Someone wants something I have.'

'Why look here?'

'They tried everywhere else.'

'But why here?'

'They must've seen me come here the other night.'

He didn't speak for a moment, his eyes studying me carefully. 'Didn't you hide it here?' he asked.

'No.'

He weighed my answer and then slowly nodded his head. 'You'd better be telling the truth,' he said.

I tried not to look too relieved. 'I am,' I said.

He grunted and came further into the room. 'Where are they?' he asked.

For a moment I wasn't sure what he meant.

'Who?'

'The men who did this. Where are they?'

'I don't know.'

He scowled. 'You said . . .'

'I haven't seen them, I don't know their names or where they come from.'

'You can find out.' It wasn't a question but I answered him.

'Yes, I can. Give me a few hours.'

'We'll be ready,' he growled.

I swallowed uneasily. It looked as if I'd got the protection I'd failed to get earlier. The trouble was it wouldn't be nicely controlled protection.

The front door opened. 'That'll be Stan,' Little Sidney said. 'I'll talk to him. You clear off.'

I nodded and waited until he had led his brother up the stairs. Big Eric came outside with me. He raised his eyebrows, in a this-way, that-way question.

'I'm going to the hospital. A friend of mine is there. She's been in some trouble.'

He pointed back to the house.

'Yes, that kind of trouble.'

He shook his head and clicked his tongue. I definitely wasn't in favour.

'I'll see you soon,' I said.

He shook his head, pointed at the ground in a peremptory manner and went back into the house. I waited.

When he came out again he had on his overcoat, a cut-down donkey-jacket. It seemed he planned on keeping me company.

I drove back to the city. I hadn't asked the young policeman where Carole would be taken but I decided to try the Royal Infirmary and I knew I'd guessed right when I saw the bulky figure of Inspector Gostelow. I thought about avoiding him but he spotted me and my chance disappeared.

'Baxter. At this rate you soon won't have any friends left.'

'It looks that way.'

'Haven't you had enough yet?'

'Meaning?'

'Meaning why don't you tell me all you know.'

'In return for which, I get what?'

'I might be persuaded not to push any charges.'

I laughed at him. 'Charges? I haven't done anything. In case you've been asleep for the past few days I'm the one who was beaten up in the car-park, and at the circus. I'm the one whose room was ripped up.' I gestured around me at the hospital. 'It's my friend who's here after a beating. It's her room that was wrecked and...' I stopped. I had been about to refer to what had happened at Big Eric's, but that was something Gostelow didn't know and it was in my interest to keep him from knowing.

'You've done something, Baxter.'

'What?'

He glared at me but didn't speak for a moment. 'Alright,' he said eventually. 'Have it your way.'

He turned to walk away but I stopped him. 'I take it you're protecting the girl against a repetition of what happened tonight?'

'Why should I?'

'It's what you're paid for.'

He took a long step forward and leaned into me. 'I don't get paid to look after half-arsed petty criminals like you,' he snarled. 'Do you know what goes on in this division? Do you know how many incidents it handles? How many people, normal respectable citizens, live here? And do you know how many men we have to cover it with? No, you don't care. All you care about is number one.'

'You're the one who started following me around,' I said, quietly, not wanting to anger the big man any more than he was.

'I did that because I thought there was something odd going on. I still think so but I'm no longer interested. As far as I'm concerned you can all beat yourselves into exhaustion. Just so long as you don't involve normal people.'

'She's normal,' I said.

'Who? The Dixon woman? She's a whore and a drunk. If you think that's normal then God knows what you think is abnormal.' He pulled his head away from me and walked heavily along the corridor. I watched him go, feeling an irrational anger at his crude description of Carole. I wanted to shout something back in her defence but then I forced myself to relax. Leaping to the defence of someone else was not my style and I didn't want to create a precedent. All the same I realised that the way things were going I would soon have to make a decision about Carole. With the prospect of being a rich man and the choice of companionship that would bring, I had a feeling the decision, when I reached it, wouldn't be in her favour.

Big Eric tugged at my sleeve and I looked down at him. He seemed excited about something but after a few abortive attempts to understand him I shook my head. 'Sorry, I can't pick it up. Look, I want to go up and see Carole. You wait here.'

He shook his head agitatedly and made some gestures I did understand.

'Okay, come with me then.'

Carole was in the bed at the end of the ward with a screen drawn around her. We were allowed in after the duty sister had indicated that we were only there because she felt it might do the girl more good than harm to see a friendly face for a few minutes. I leaned over the bed and touched her hand. She opened her eyes and managed a smile. The swellings and bruises looked much worse in those clean surroundings than they had in her room.

'I'm sorry,' I said.

She shook her head. 'Not your fault,' she whispered.

'It was.'

She shook her head again and tried a smile. 'Mine.' She turned her head as Big Eric moved silently round to the other side of the bed and then quickly turned her head away again before he could see her damaged face.

'It's only Big Eric,' I said. 'I told you about him.'

She nodded but kept her face averted from him. 'I'm sorry they smashed your stereo equipment.'

I shrugged. 'Easy come, easy go.' She knew how much I'd paid for it all, a great deal of money by our standards.

'I'm sorry,' she said again, tears forming in her eyes and beginning to roll down her inflamed cheeks.

'Don't,' I said and took her hands and held them for a few minutes, neither of us speaking, until the sister quietly entered the screened-off area around the bed.

'You can come back tomorrow, you know,' she said.

'When is visiting time?'

'Don't worry about that. Did you know she'd put you down as next of kin?'

'No,' I said.

'Isn't it right?'

I thought for a moment. 'I suppose it is,' I said. 'In a manner of speaking, that is.'

We reached the main exit before Big Eric stopped me. He looked at me and there was an expression there I hadn't seen before. He pointed upwards.

'Carole?'

He nodded.

'What about her?'

He pointed at my mouth.

I knew what that meant. I had to repeat what I'd said last. 'Carole.'

He nodded and made a continuing movement with one hand.

'Carole Dixon?'

A nod.

'Her name means something?'

Another nod. Then he made sweeping and darting gestures over his body and arms and legs finishing with a series of pricking movements with one finger against the back of his other hand.

I had a sinking feeling that I knew what he was trying to tell me. 'The tattooed man?'

I was right. He pointed upwards again.

'Carole and the tattooed man?'

He nodded.

'She was the pretty girl who was with him in Bristol?'

A nod.

Christ, I thought. I should have known. I pulled a thought out of my subconscious and recalled the conversation we'd had when she had been unusually curious about Jenks and the fact that Big Eric had seen him in Bristol.

'Thanks.'

He pulled at my sleeve.

'More?'

A nod, followed by the continuing gesture.

'Carole Dixon.'

A nod then he made a writing movement and followed it with the tattooing sign.

'That was his name? Jenks was called Dixon when you knew him?'

He nodded and beamed. I leaned against the corridor wall feeling like Chico must've felt after half a dozen takes with Harpo.

'Any more?' I asked him.

He shook his head, pleased, but then the smile faded as he saw I didn't look at all happy about it.

'Not what I expected,' I said. 'Thanks all the same, mate.'

I straightened up and we went out into the night air. Apart from the little matter of whose side B.J. Williams was on I seemed to have most of the answers. All that remained was for me to engineer an appropriate finale and I would be clear and away with a packet of money and a small fortune in diamonds. No woman though. I didn't seem to have the right touch when it came to choosing bedmates.

CHAPTER FOURTEEN

I took Big Eric back home. He wanted me to go in but I didn't feel up to facing an inquisition from his three sons. In any event I had more pressing business. I told him I would either call round or telephone when I needed him and the lads.

I watched him shuffle up the garden path, his black plimsolls making no sound, his tiny figure almost lost in the dark shadows cast by the high, unclipped, privet hedge. I let in the clutch and drove away slowly.

Until I could talk again to Carole there were a lot of unanswered questions, but a few things were becoming clearer. I now knew how the tattooed man had known about me, how he'd got my name and telephone number, how he'd known which was my car. The package of diamonds hadn't been dropped accidentally or for him to collect later, he'd dropped it for Carole and she had replaced it with the package containing six thousand pounds. I didn't know, but I could guess that Claude Jenks was carrying a consignment of stones that were either stolen or smuggled, or both. Carole was the next link in the chain, but someone must have been on to him and he hadn't wanted to point the finger at her, so they'd picked on me as an unwitting post office.

I now understood the need for the charade at the pub when he had gone to great lengths to ensure everyone noticed him. It had been a bluff, a double-bluff. He knew that anyone he met, like me, would be suspect but, by behaving outrageously, he would make anyone watching him think I wasn't involved. At least until he and Carole had time to make the switch. Once that was done and he'd met me at the library and collected the money he would be away. Carole would have passed on the diamonds and it wouldn't matter, then, if I was leaned on, because I wouldn't have anything and I wouldn't know anything.

Only it hadn't worked that way, something Jenks could never have foreseen happened. He had a heart-attack and died. Even then things could have gone on much as he'd planned, but I'd screwed it up by finding both the diamonds and the money.

I could see why I wasn't very popular with a lot of people. I was sure I had most of them pegged. The two men who had beaten me up at the Hastings and the fortune-teller had been watching Jenks. They were the people he was afraid to lead to Carole.

The two men in the circus tent were a separate team, probably Jenks' partners, maybe the next link in the chain. They certainly knew what Carole had put into my car. I remembered the first set of bruises she'd displayed. Perhaps she had been forced into telling them about that.

That left B. J. Williams and Joe Cornwell, the actor, to fit into the scheme of things. And the cornet-player. I wasn't completely certain he was tied in with the fortune-teller. Her reaction when I'd talked to her hadn't been quite right.

I hadn't progressed much further when I reached the house where B.J. had her flat. I parked the car and felt in my pocket for the key to her bedroom door. I went up the path and in through the front door with a minimum of juggling with my faithful plastic calendar. I did the same with her flat door and walked over to the bedroom door and listened. Everything was quiet. I slipped the key into the lock, turned it and opened the door.

The long, flowing, dress that had done so much for my blood pressure was still on the bed, but there was no sign of its owner. I made sure no-one was lurking behind the door waiting to bounce some heavy object on my head and switched on the light. I crossed to the window and looked for some sign of how she had managed to get out but there was nothing to suggest she'd gone that way. If she had, she'd managed to fasten the window behind her and fasten it on the inside too. I had a vaguely unsettled feeling, it was too much the classic, locked-room mystery for my liking.

I stood there, worrying about it, then heard a faint clattering sound. I didn't know the layout of the other flats in the old house so there was a good chance the sound had come from one of them, but I couldn't be sure. The cassette-holder I'd taken from Carole's room suddenly seemed red-hot. I looked hastily around the room for a likely hiding place. After a moment I came to the conclusion that nowhere was very safe, but, provided I could get back to it fairly soon, under the mattress might be the best. I took the cassette-holder out of my pocket and, lifting the edge of the mattress, slipped it underneath. I went out of the bedroom, crossed to the kitchen, opened the door and looked in. Nothing there seemed out of place and I started to turn away. Then I remembered the telephone I'd dropped into the pedal-bin and turned back to get it. I went into that room with less care than I'd shown when I had gone into the bedroom. Much less care.

I caught a smell, perfume, after-shave, pleasant anyway, and then something crashed onto the back of my head. I had a mildly appreciative thought that the blow hadn't landed on the same side as the last crack I'd taken and then everything went pleasingly black and I slid down to the floor.

When I came round my first sensation was one of well-being and comfort, feelings that faded rapidly when I tried to move my head and it threatened to come apart and which disappeared entirely when I opened my eyes and saw, sitting in the chair directly in front of me, the looming bulk of Detective Inspector Gostelow.

'You're alive, then,' he remarked, with almost total disinterest.

'I'm not sure. Maybe I died and went to the other place.'

He smiled faintly. 'Anything's possible.'

'Am I allowed to ask what happened, or will that sound too much like a line from a bad movie?'

'How disappointing. I thought you were going to tell me what happened.'

I looked around me for the first time. B.J. Williams' flat looked the way it had before. I was sitting on a long, brown velvet settee, Gostelow was threatening to overwhelm a matching armchair and the young constable, who had accompanied me around the town and whom I'd left in Carole's room earlier, was hovering uncertainly in a corner.

'Somebody hit me,' I said.

'How original.'

'True all the same.'

'Mm.'

'It is.'

'I'm not disputing it, Baxter. You were lying on the kitchen floor with a lump behind your ear

184

I don't think was put there by any of your other recent activities.'

'So, why the inquisition?'

He waved a thick arm at the room. 'Is this yours? It isn't, is it?'

'It belongs to a friend.'

'Ah.'

'Ask him,' I pointed at the constable. 'I came here earlier tonight and I was with the woman who owns it.'

'I have had the constable's report. I am aware of your activities.'

'Well, then.'

'So what? You were here earlier, with the owner. You're here now, without. You haven't got a key to the place on your person so you effected entry by other means.'

'Maybe she left the door open for me.'

His eyes narrowed slightly. 'Is that what you're going to say?'

'When?'

'When we put you in court.'

'Charged with what?'

'I imagine you know the complexities of the housebreaking and burglary laws as well as I do,' he said. 'There are enough hooks in it to cover this little exercise.'

'Nothing has been taken,' I said.

'Perhaps not.'

'You can ask her.'

There was a pause. 'No doubt I can,' he said.

I looked across to the kitchen and bedroom doors. Both were closed. 'Where is she?' I asked.

He didn't answer that one at all and we sat looking at each other in silence for several minutes before he heaved his bulk up out of the arm-chair and leaned over me. 'I'll ask the question once,' he said. 'What happened?'

'Search me.'

'Alright, let's do that.'

I looked at him for a moment to see if he meant it. He did. I stood up unsteadily and emptied my pockets. There was nothing there that was of any interest to him. 'See,' I said. 'Me no stealee.'

'Very amusing.'

'So what are you going to charge me with?'

'I'll think of something. When it suits me.'

I had a sinking feeling he meant it and, while I could very probably fight it successfully, it wasn't the way I'd planned to spend my time after I had turned the diamonds into cash.

I tried a thought aloud. 'Always assuming the owner of this place wants to go to all that trouble, when nothing has been taken.'

He didn't like that. 'Miss Williams is ...'

'A very good friend of mine,' I finished for him.

From the bedroom the telephone started to ring. The constable had gone in to answer it before it registered on my battered brain that the last time I'd seen the telephone it had been in the pedal-bin in the kitchen. The call was for Gostelow and I sat listening to his rumbling voice from behind the door he had carefully closed.

'How did you know I was here?' I asked the constable.

'We had a . . .' He broke off, aware that I was a suspicious character and wasn't supposed to be treated like a human-being. It didn't matter, he'd told me enough. They'd had a telephone call. The call must have been made by whoever had hit me. It didn't make a lot of sense.

Gostelow came back into the room and jerked a thumb at me. 'Get out.'

'Eh?'

He glowered at me. 'I'd like to throw you in a cell and leave you to fester.'

'Then why. . .?'

'Just get out, Baxter.'

I can take a hint. I got out.

I climbed into the Cortina and started the engine. I waited for a moment or two to see if anyone was taking an interest in me. It seemed they were not, which suited me perfectly well.

I drove slowly back to Big Eric's house. Food, a few hours sleep, then instructions to the troops and I reckoned I would be ready, as ready as I ever would be, to make myself a fortune.

Big Eric's three sons were sitting in the small living-room, their collective bulk making it seem even more cramped than usual.

They all looked at me with expressions several degrees colder than their customary indifference.

'How is she?' I asked.

'Better than she was,' Little Sidney volunteered, grudgingly.

'Can I go up and see her?'

'Dad's up there.'

'I'll wait,' I said.

'That's what we're doing,' Joey said.

I knew what he meant.

'Not much longer,' I said.

'How long?'

'Tomorrow afternoon, about five.'

'Why wait until then?'

'Because I have to do something first and anyway, it will be getting dark by then and that will help.'

'Help who? Us or you?' Little Sidney wasn't prepared to let me off the hook so easily.

'All of us,' I said. 'We don't want to end up in prison over it, do we?'

'As long as I get the buggers who did this I don't care.'

I looked around the room. There was little sign left of what had happened, but I didn't say so. 'Your mum wouldn't like it,' I said instead.

He grunted, but I could tell he agreed. The Perkins family had never had trouble with the law and they didn't intend starting now.

'Alright,' Stan said, speaking for the first time. 'Five o'clock. What are you cooking up now?'

'There are two parties in this,' I said. 'At the moment I'm not absolutely certain which one did this, but I expect to find out.'

'What do we do?'

'I'll go to the Fair about two. I'll set up a meeting for five, then I'll leave the fairground and sit in my car. I'll park in Albert Avenue. You two,' I pointed to Little Sidney and Stan. 'You leave here at four. Will you use your bike?'

'Yes.'

'Right, drop Stan at the Anlaby Road end of Albert Avenue then come down Albert Avenue until you see me. When you do, make sure I know you're there. Use your horn, but don't make a production out of it, in case someone's watching me. I don't want anyone to know we're together.'

'Okay, you don't have to spell it out.'

'What do I do?' Stan asked.

'When Little Sidney drops you off, walk to the fairground and wander around for a while, I want you near a particular caravan by, say, ten minutes to five.' I told them where the fortune-teller's caravan was located.

'What do I do after I've seen you in your car?' Little Sidney asked.

'Find somewhere to park the bike then go into the Fair from the Spring Bank end and do

189

the same as Stan.'

'What will you be doing?'

'At about ten to five I'll come into the fairground and go straight to the caravan. I'll be inside, oh, maybe ten minutes. When I come out, unless I tell you otherwise, drift over to the Big Wheel.'

'Why can't we go straight there?'

'In case there's a change in plans.'

'You mean in case you run into trouble,' Little Sidney said. He was close to the truth.

'What about me?' Joey asked.

'Make your own way to the fairground and be outside the Ghost Train by five. After I've left the caravan I'll come that way round. You pick me up there. Follow me, keep far enough back so no-one connects us, but be ready in case there's any trouble.'

'What kind of trouble?'

'Any kind.'

They chewed it over for a while.

'When do we get at them?' Little Sidney said eventually.

'When I tell you who's responsible,' I said.

They didn't seem too happy with it and I could see what worried them. They knew I was up to something but couldn't work out what it was. I didn't care, all I wanted was protection in case anyone tried to jump me before I reached the Big Wheel. After that I would be on my own.

The door opened and Big Eric came in. He grinned at me, pointed upwards and delivered a thumb's up.

'Can I go up?'

He nodded.

Doris was sitting up in bed and I was pleased to see her face was back to its usual bright red.

'I feel a fraud,' she said.

'Why?'

'I'm perfectly well, I should be down there but they won't let me.'

'It won't do them any harm.'

Her face clouded for an instant. 'They're going to try to find the men who did this, aren't they?'

'Yes.'

'Can you stop them?'

I shook my head, not wanting to risk speaking. I didn't know if my conscience would allow me to get away with it. I had used her, I was using her sons and I planned to use her husband again.

'Oh well. They're grown men, I suppose.'

'What, er, where did you hide the package?'

She smiled at that. 'It's in the kitchen. The cupboard beside the cooker. There's a pile of cake tins. It's in the bottom one.'

'Thanks,' I said.

'It's valuable, isn't it?'

'Yes.'

'I hope it's worth what you're doing to

yourself.'

That sounded like another piece of psychology. 'I think so.'

I left her and went down to the living-room. The lads had gone, some adrenalin must have been generated now they knew that action wasn't far away. Big Eric glanced enquiringly at me.

'Can you do something for me?' I asked.

He nodded.

'Do you know any of the Bingo stall men?'

A nod.

I told him what I wanted and he looked puzzled but nodded and pointed at the clock on the mantelpiece.

'As soon as you can.'

He made a circular movement.

'An hour?'

He nodded and went out.

I waited a few minutes then went into the kitchen and opened the cupboard door. Half a dozen cake tins were stacked, one inside the other, ready for Doris's next baking session. I lifted them out, one at a time. The package was in the bottom of the biggest tin, completely hidden by the tins above it. I took it out and went back into the living room. I rang directory enquiries and asked for the number of a hotel I knew in the centre of Manchester. Then I rang the hotel, gave them a false name and booked a room for the middle of the following week. I told them I was expecting a small package through the post and they should keep it for me to collect. Then I rooted around for a ballpoint pen and readdressed the package to me care of the hotel.

I went out and walked to the nearest post-box which had a stamp machine and stuck on more than enough stamps. I didn't think the hotel could be relied upon to pay the postage if I tried the stampless routine I'd used the first time. I dropped the parcel into the box with a slight feeling of loss but I knew the risks would be much greater if I kept the money on me or even tried to find another hiding place for it.

Then I went back to the house, made a pot of tea and carried a cup upstairs to Doris. She was fretting to be up and about but I made her sit back in her bed and drink the tea. I talked casually about the men who had come to the house but she hadn't seen either of them, she'd been attacked from behind and neither of them had spoken, something that had seemed the most frightening aspect of the whole affair to her. She was certain there had been two of them, from the noises they'd made as they searched the house but, although I didn't say anything to her, that didn't help me a lot. It could have been the two from the car-park of the Hastings or it could have been the bald-headed man with the soft voice and his hairy friend.

'They were after your package, weren't they?'

she asked.

'There wasn't any point in telling her lies. 'Yes.'

'I'd better not tell the boys that.'

Boys! They'd tear me apart if they knew I was behind it. 'Not if you want me to stay in one piece,' I agreed.

'You're a bad lad, Johnny.'

'If you mean I'm looking after myself, then you're right.'

'Whatever it costs?'

That sounded like a deep question and it wasn't one I wanted to think about. 'No,' I said.

'Are you sure?'

She wasn't letting go. With three big sons, permanent children in the sense that she was still feeding them and washing their clothes, to say nothing of coping with being married to a roving circus-rigger who was also mute, she should have had enough on her plate without worrying about me. But, as the only woman in my life of a similar age to the mother I had never known, she seemed to think she had some responsibility for my welfare. She hadn't, but I didn't have the heart to say so.

'Sure enough,' I answered her question.

She snorted disbelief and disapproval in equal proportions. 'You use people, Johnny.'

We'd never had that particular line before, in our infrequent sorties about my way of life, and I wasn't too sure I liked the way it was pointing.

'Sometimes, maybe,' I admitted cautiously.

'Most of the time and there's no maybe about it.'

'Come on, Doris,' I said, trying to think of a polite way to end the conversation.

'You could've tried harder with Sandra.'

I didn't like that line either but it seemed safer, much less close to my present problems. 'Perhaps I could have done more but, when Sandra left me, it seemed the best way out so I just let it happen.'

'That poor girl.'

'Sandra?'

'Her too, but I meant Susie.'

'She doesn't seem to miss me. Not now...' I stopped.

'Not now that her mother's made you out to be the villain of the piece,' Doris finished for me.

'Something like that.'

'She needs a father, even one like you.'

'She'll be getting one if Sandra remarries.'

'That won't last.'

As long as it gets off the ground it will suit me, I thought. One more thing off my back although, with luck, I would soon be far enough away not to have to worry anymore about my ex-wife and child. They were responsibilities I no longer wanted and which I'd never been able to take seriously enough anyway. I decided to leave behind a large enough amount of cash to keep them free from worry, not for ever, but at least until lover-boy got a job and married Sandra. It would be safe enough, Sandra would keep the sudden acquisition of cash very quiet indeed— just in case she suspected it wasn't quite legal. Her disapproval of my life style wouldn't be strong enough to make her pass up anything like that. I felt mildly pleased at my generosity and tried hard not to notice the sudden, unexpected tug at the thought that, soon, even the infrequent visits to see them would stop. Not that I cared whether I ever saw Sandra but Susie was a different matter.

'Maybe she'll be lucky this time,' I said.

'Let's hope so. I can't say I like her all that much, but she certainly doesn't deserve two bad marriages.'

'Yes, well, drink that up before it gets cold.'

She sipped the rest of her tea and I took the cup from her and stood up.

'Be careful,' she told me.

'See, you still worry about me,' I said, lightly.

'Somebody has to.'

I went out of her room and down the stairs. I washed the tea cups and then sat on a stool in the kitchen and thought about the round, usually cheerful, little woman upstairs. I came to the conclusion that I might very well miss her more than anyone when I left. I would have to find some way of showing what I thought, felt, about her. It would have to be something special. I tried to think of some suitable gift but after a while I gave up. She didn't seem to need anything, certainly nothing I could buy.

I went through into the front room and settled down to wait for Big Eric. After a while it occurred to me that the best present I could give Doris would be the news that I had settled down into what she would think of as a normal life. A home of my own, a new wife, more children, only this time on a permanent basis. Somehow it didn't seem very likely that I would ever be able to give her that kind of news.

CHAPTER FIFTEEN

I arrived at the fairground shortly after two o'clock the following afternoon and, without making any attempt to shuffle in unnoticed, went directly to the fortune-teller's caravan. A sign on the door announced that she wouldn't be there until the evening. I knocked anyway and after a few seconds she opened the door.

'Got the money?' I asked.

'Not here,' she said, guardedly.

'But you're ready to do the deal?'

'Yes.'

'Five o'clock.'

'Very well,' she said.

I turned away and then glanced over my

shoulder at her. She had a gleam in her eye that was hastily dimmed when she saw me looking at her. Maybe she was busy reading my future.

I walked out of the fairground and along the road to where I'd parked the car and climbed in. I slipped a cassette into the deck and lay back in the seat. I had nowhere to go until Little Sidney arrived, and sitting in the car in broad daylight on a public road seemed a safe place to be. I'd picked out a cassette that suited my mildly euphoric mood and did Johnny Hodges a grave disservice by dozing off halfway through it.

Little Sidney announced his arrival, as I'd told him to, with a discreet bleep from the horn of the Honda. I didn't acknowledge his signal.

After half an hour I locked the car and walked to the fairground. The fortune-teller still hadn't taken down her sign. I glanced around before knocking on the door. Little Sidney was rolling coins with the expression of a man who would become rather angry if he didn't win something. He glanced up and saw me but I turned away before he could acknowledge my presence.

The door opened almost immediately and I went in. She was alone.

'Okay?'

'Yes,' she said and indicated a plastic carrier-bag on the table.

I reached out, opened it and looked inside. There was a brown-paper wrapped bundle in it.

'Do I need to count it?'

'Suit yourself.'

I shrugged. 'Like you said, I have to trust you.'

'You have the diamonds?'

'Not on me.'

Her eyes narrowed. 'I hope you're not planning something, Baxter. I wouldn't advise it.'

'Don't worry. I'll be back with the stones in half an hour, but not here. Meet me by the Big Wheel. We'll make the swap there.'

'The place will be swarming with people.'

'Precisely.'

'It's dangerous.'

'Why is it? Two people exchanging a package for a plastic carrier-bag. What could be more innocent than that?'

'Do you think I'm a fool?'

'You mean I'm not giving you a chance to check that the stones really are in my package?'

'Yes.'

I pretended to think about it. 'Okay,' I said. 'Tell you what. We'll meet there and take a ride on the Wheel. While we're up there you can check the stones and I'll count the money. How does that sound?'

She didn't like it. 'I'm not sure.'

'Do you want to talk to your friend again?'

'I . . . yes.'

'Of course, you could always send your boss.'

She didn't like that either. 'In half an hour at

the Big Wheel,' she said.

'Half an hour,' I agreed and left the caravan.

When I reached the circus tent I went round to the back and into the non-public part where the animals were kept between shows. I saw Big Eric busily fixing a bell-covered harness to an elephant.

I went over to him. 'Got it?'

He looked down from the top of a pair of wooden steps that were propped against the elephant's right foreleg. He nodded, dived a hand into his pocket and came out with a small packet. I took it and placed it in my own pocket. He looked anxious.

'Don't worry,' I said. 'Everything's under control.'

He didn't look convinced.

'You've set things up with the generator man?'

He nodded.

'Thanks,' I said.

He still looked concerned.

'I know what I'm doing,' I assured him.

He raised an eyebrow and then the grin came back and he showed me an upturned thumb.

'I'll see you later,' I told him and left him there hurriedly finishing festooning the elephant with the jingling bells.

I reached the Big Wheel a couple of minutes inside the half hour I'd stipulated. I leaned against the huge, throbbing generator and

200

looked at the faces of the milling crowd, faces lit by the profusion of lights. My ears began to ache with the noise from the generator, the yells and shrieks of girls and young men, who were enjoying being scared out of their wits, and the amplified music from loudspeakers was spilling out different sounds as one attraction vied with another, ageing Bay City Roller's records mixing with ageless Rolling Stones' numbers.

I spotted Big Eric's three sons easily enough. They were trying to look casual but not succeeding very well. They were too eager to get their collective hands on the thugs who had turned over their home, to be calm.

Then I noticed two other men looking too casual to be true. I couldn't be sure but I was prepared to gamble they were the men who had attacked me in the car-park of the Hastings. Another minute went by and then I spotted the thick-set man who had knelt on my neck in the circus tent. I let my eyes rove across the faces closest to him and in a moment or two I saw his eagle-nosed, bald companion.

Everything seemed to be going well. All that was needed was the fortune-teller with her bag full of money.

'Hello, dear. Fancy meeting a boy like you in a place like this.'

The voice was within inches of my ear and I spun round in surprise. It was Philip Jason. He looked different in a hairy tweed overcoat, heavier, somehow bigger and, apart from the voice, not in the least bit effeminate.

'I'm trying to see this lot with your artistic eyes,' I said.

'How nice,' he replied. He looked around him. 'Of course,' he went on. 'There is a disadvantage in seeing it from this viewpoint. Too close to the ground, too much noise, too many smells. Altogether too many distractions.'

'I expect you're right,' I said.

'Much better from up there.' He glanced upwards at the Big Wheel which was slowly filling up, one chair at a time, as it moved spasmodically, each movement bringing another chair to the ground where its passengers could clamber off to be replaced by other eager youngsters.

'No doubt,' I said.

'Do you fancy a little spin, dear?'

I looked at him, a thought forming at the back of my mind. 'I'm waiting for a friend.'

He sighed. 'That's the story of my life.' Then his voice changed fractionally. 'Perhaps I could be your friend.'

I looked at him, puzzled. The words didn't suit the new hardness in his voice. 'You?'

'Me.'

'Then . . .'

'I have what you want. I take it you have what I want.'

I nodded slowly. 'I've got them.'

'Good, let's go for a spin shall we.' His voice had changed back again and he turned away towards the queue. Something must have passed between him and the man taking the money at the wire gate because we queue-jumped, to the annoyance of those waiting. I didn't look behind me as I went through the gate but I heard angry voices that grew louder. I guessed we were not the only ones jumping the queue.

Jason climbed into the chair and I followed. As soon as we were seated the attendant swung the safety bar into place, pressed his button and we swung forward and upwards until the next chair was in position. Then the next. Then one more. The next time he pressed the button we didn't stop but began the first slow, full revolution.

When we reached the top, Jason gripped my arm and pointed outwards with a theatrical gesture. 'See,' he said, his head close to mine. 'A beautiful sight.'

I looked down. He was right, it was. From up there all that could be seen were the coloured lights and the tinselly brightness of the fair. The sounds that floated up were mainly musical, the shrill crowd noise becoming a muted, background hum.

'Very pretty,' I said.

'But not as pretty as some sights I imagine you would rather see.'

'True.'

'You're a materialist, Mr. Baxter.'

'What are you?'

'Sadly, I begin to think, as I grow older, there is more of the materialist in me than I like to acknowledge.'

'Which means?'

He glanced sideways. We were almost at the bottom of the revolution and I could see the three sons of Doris Perkins standing close to the wire safety-fence. None of them looked very happy. I couldn't see any sign of the others I had spotted before Jason had spoken to me. I guessed they were somewhere behind me on the Wheel but I didn't look. I wasn't supposed to know they were there.

We were well on the way to the top again before Jason answered my question. 'It means I'm ready to do business.'

'Show me.'

He reached under his coat and pulled out a plastic carrier-bag. His apparent plumpness vanished. The bag looked like the one I'd seen in the caravan. I took it from him and opened it.

'The stones,' he said.

'One thing at a time.'

'The stones,' he repeated.

'I can't run away,' I said, reasonably. I reached into the bag and opened the inner wrapping. The contents seemed perfectly satisfactory. I pulled out a few notes at random and they all looked good, although in that light they could easily have been forgeries. I didn't think that was likely. In the time they'd had, finding the genuine article would have been troublesome enough, producing that many reasonably good quality forged notes would have been impossible.

I put the carrier down on the floor of the chair and took out of my pocket the packet Big Eric had given me in the circus tent and handed it over to Jason.

He opened it up and took out a little bag. As we went up again, Jason carefully slackened the drawstrings of the bag and peered in. Then he shook the bag and two or three stones trickled into his palm. The light reflected from the coloured lamps along the spars of the Big Wheel caught them and threw out a sparkle of reflected brilliance. It looked as if Big Eric's friend from the Bingo stall had done him proud. For a moment even I thought they looked like the real thing.

'This isn't the best place to examine diamonds,' Jason said.

'What else could they be?' I asked, innocently.

He glanced at me and then slowly nodded his head. 'No, I don't suppose you've had either the time or the opportunity to have copies made.'

'I wouldn't know where to go to have copies made,' I said, truthfully enough.

We were at the top again when the circular

movement of the Wheel stopped and we hung there, the chair rocking slowly. I leaned sideways and looked down. We didn't appear to be stopping to let anyone off. I brought my eyes towards the operator and I could just make out a woman, who could have been the fortune-teller, standing next to him. At that height I could have been wrong, but I was sure I wasn't. Jason needed time to make a switch of the carrier-bag containing the money and it would have been her job to ensure he had the time to do it and their heavyweight mates were on the Wheel in case I tried to leave by helicopter. I felt a movement beside me and then Jason was still again. I turned back, reached down and picked up the carrier and fingered the top. Jason tensed, then I pushed the bag inside my anorak and he relaxed again. It all seemed to be working out well enough. I'd got one team onto the Wheel by inviting them there. I'd expected the fortune-teller to come with the two heavies not, I admit, Philip Jason. I hadn't figured him for the boss. Come to that, I hadn't figured him for anything but a pansified theatrical producer. That should've warned me that taking people at face value was a dangerous game but it hadn't.

The other team, the two who had beaten me up in the circus tent, were there because I'd guessed, correctly it seemed, that they would be keeping a watchful eye on Big Eric as a lead to me. I'd asked him to convey to one of his mates, a talkative man who did some simple task, like cleaning out the lions' cage, and who also managed to hold conversations with Big Eric, that some kind of bent deal would be taking place on the Big Wheel. I'd told Big Eric to encourage the talkative lion-man to spread the word. Once the two men heard about it I guessed they'd be able to fill in the details without much difficulty. I calculated they would let the whole thing proceed as I'd planned it. That way they would have an opportunity to get back their diamonds, a packet of cash into the bargain and, as an added bonus, they would be able to get a crack at the opposition. Something I imagined was just as important to them as anything else.

All that remained was for Big Eric to ring up the curtain on the final act. At that moment, right on cue, he did so . All the lights on the Big Wheel went out.

I turned to Jason. 'What's happening?' I asked, before he had a chance to speak.

I guessed he was trying to work out if I was responsible and, if so, to what end. Then he gave up because, as we were up there together, it would seem to him there was no way I could gain an advantage.

'Probably a power failure,' he said, stating the obvious.

'Probably,' I agreed. 'You don't look the type for this kind of thing,' I went on, conversationally.

'Is there a type?'

'Probably not,' I conceded. 'But if there was you wouldn't be it.' I leaned over the side again and peered into the darkness. 'Who's in the chair below us?' I asked.

'What?'

'Your lady friend is down below isn't she? So who came up with us? The heavies who tried it on in the car-park?'

After a moment he decided there was no point in pretending otherwise. 'Yes,' he said. 'They' are there.'

'To stop me from trying anything?'

'A reasonable precaution.'

'Except they can't see us from where they are.'

He fidgeted uneasily. 'No, they can't.'

'Of course, if you'd remembered the wheel went this way round and not the other, they would be ahead of us, not behind, and I would be a sitting target. As it is, they've wasted their admission money.'

'Perhaps.'

'No perhaps about it, Jason.'

'You are not planning anything foolish, I hope.'

'No more than you.'

'What does that mean?'

I pulled out the carrier bag and held it to him. 'Shall we have another look at the contents of this, or do you want me to guess what's in it?'

He didn't answer and it was too dark to see the expression on his face. 'What do you want?' he asked, eventually.

'Let's start with the money.'

He hesitated and then, no doubt calculating that I couldn't get very far before his thugs would be after me, he slowly reached under his coat and pulled out the duplicate bag.

'I didn't think you would try a switch on me,' I said, trying to sound as if I meant it.

'You can't blame me for trying,' he said.

I took the bag and carefully placed it with the duplicate, taking care I remembered which was which. 'Now the diamonds,' I said.

'Wh . . .'

'The diamonds,' I repeated.

'You won't . . .'

'Don't tell me what I will or won't do, Jason,' I said. 'Just give me the diamonds.'

Very slowly he took the small bag out of his pocket and handed it to me. Cautiously I fiddled the top open and looked inside.

'Just to make sure you haven't made another switch,' I said, to cover the fact that there wasn't any need for me to open the top. Then I half-turned from him and sent up a small prayer that he would try something. He did.

He grabbed at me and, with a mild sensation of relief, I threw up one hand as if in alarm. It was the hand holding the bag of stones and even in the near-darkness we both saw the stones fly out of the bag and disappear into the crowd below.

'My God,' Jason said softly. 'You fool, Baxter, you bloody fool.'

'Christ,' I said, with appropriate emotion.

He slumped back into the chair. 'The money,' he said after a moment.

'What about it?'

'Hand it back.'

'Sorry, that's mine as well.'

'Oh, no.'

'Oh, yes.'

'You can't get away with it.'

'Guess again,' I said. I stood up and the chair rocked violently. 'I'll be seeing you,' I said.

I stepped over the edge of the chair and swung myself down, my feet searching for a touch on one of the spars. Above me I heard Jason yelling at his henchmen in the next chair. He had a louder voice than I'd expected, which was just as well. There wouldn't be any doubt that the two men in the next chair beyond would hear him too. I eased my way onto the spar until I felt a cross-member I could brace against. Then I stopped and shuffled the two plastic bags, ready for the next part of the performance.

Unfortunately the fine drizzle that had fallen most of the day had thoroughly soaked the steel framework and, without any warning at all, my foot slipped and I felt myself fall outwards into black space.

CHAPTER SIXTEEN

Everyone is entitled to at least one brush with death and that was when I had mine. Instinct, sharpened by years of working high above the ground took over, while conscious thought was worrying about mundanities like trying to hold onto two plastic bags, one of which held twenty thousand pounds.

It wasn't that I wanted the money. I didn't. It wasn't part of the plan that I should keep it. But it had to be disposed of in the right way otherwise I would still have a problem. A problem! There I was, on the brink of falling almost a hundred feet to certain death, and I thought the bag of money was the problem.

Fortunately my instincts were a little more realistic than my brain. As I swung through the air, my feet still hooked into the latticed steelwork, I used that point of contact as a fulcrum and kept swinging until I saw the black spidery steel of a lower part of the frame in front of me. I grabbed at it, one-handed, my concern over the money still fighting to be heard, and took a grip. I was safe. Upside down, high above the ground and with the nearest people to me unlikely to care if I fell the rest of the way, but safe.

Hastily I scrambled down the spar until I could manoeuvre myself into a safer position and one where I was the right way up. Then I took a quick look inside the first plastic bag. It was the duplicate bag, and I jammed it into a point where two spars joined. Then, with the other bag safely hanging from my wrist, I pulled myself upright, worked my way along the frame and then stopped and looked upwards. I could see two shadowy shapes moving in the framework and I let them get a little further from their chair before I reached out for the nearest upright. It took me longer to climb up it than I'd expected. My left leg wasn't as strong as it had been but I finally made it. From my new position I was within fingertip reach of the bottom of the chair that still held Philip Jason and I could see the two men on the frame more clearly. They were both Jason's men. I looked round me and saw the chair beyond the one they had left was rocking to and fro and moments later the legs of another man came cautiously into sight. When he was fully in view I could see that he was short and stubby and I guessed it was the hairy little man who had knelt on my neck while bald-eagle questioned me.

I waited and he began to move after the first two men. Between the three of them I expected someone would soon find the plastic bag I'd left behind. One of Jason's men did so, a few seconds later. I heard him yell to his partner that he'd found it. The stubby man couldn't have missed hearing too. He began to work his way down towards the others. He was making slow progress and he appeared to be using only one hand. I didn't like to think about what he might be holding in the other hand.

I scrambled rapidly up to the next chair where I hoped to find the soft-spoken, bald-headed man who had questioned and kicked me as I lay helpless under his short, hairy, companion's knee. It would by very tempting to use the moment to settle that particular score, but I would have to resist. At least until the scenario I had planned was completed. Just before I reached the chair it occurred to me that if he wasn't there I would have to improvise an entirely new scenario. The momentary qualm passed when I saw him, leaning awkwardly over the side, trying to see what was happening beneath him. I grabbed at the toe-plate of the chair and pulled myself upwards, the whole thing rocking forward as I did so.

I saw him spin round and reach for his pocket but then I came up over the safety rail and he could see that all I had in my hands was a plastic shopping bag. He left his hand inside his coat and I let out a suitably surprised gasp of astonishment. 'You? Here?'

He smiled, his teeth gleaming briefly in the darkness. 'So, the enterpising Mr. Baxter.'

'How did you get here?' I said, glumly.

'You're not as clever as you thought you were,' he said.

Aren't I though, I thought. 'So it seems, I said.

'Where are the diamonds?'

'Gone.'

'What do you mean, gone?'

'I tried to get them back. They fell.'

He glared at me but then nodded slowly. 'I heard the shouting, I wondered what had happened. A pity but there is still the money.'

'I left that on the frame,' I said.

'I think not.'

From below I heard shouting. 'What do you think they're fighting about,' I said.

'I'm not a fool, hand over the bag.'

I shrugged and held out the bag. He reached for it and I hit him, once but hard, across the neck with the side of my hand. It was a small return for the way he and his partner had treated me. He pulled his other hand from his coat. It wasn't a gun, which helped, it was a small leather cosh. That wasn't a lot better but at least it meant he needed to grapple with me. I swung the bag round and, first time lucky, sent the cosh spinning out of his grasp. I changed my grip on the bag and swung it again. It worked like a charm. The mouth of the bag opened and banknotes flew out, in a sweeping curve, like a flock of suddenly released pigeons.

'Oh, no.' I groaned with some realism because, even in the cause of ensuring that I lived to spend a lot of money, I needed to rid myself of that particular parcel.

The man turned and stared at me. At that moment I was aware that I might have overstepped the limit of his patience. I think he would have happily killed me for no reason other than as a punishment for my stupidity.

From above and below I was suddenly aware that the night was filled with voices. It was an odd feeling, high up there in the darkness yet surrounded by the clamour of people talking and shouting. Some, who sounded like young girls, were crying and other voices, male and protective, were assuring them that all was well and the Wheel would soon be turning again.

From further below, from the ground, came a few shouts that sounded authoritative and then, as I listened, mingled with them were other cries. Cries of surprise and excitement. The first of the banknotes were reaching the ground.

The bald-headed man was still glaring at me and I looked back at him, steadily, trying not to encourage his obvious inclinations. Fortunately Big Eric's timing was again perfect. At that moment all the lights came back on to a ragged cheer from the genuine passengers on the Big Wheel. Cheers that were echoed from friends, relatives and sensation seekers down below. Cheers that suddenly changed to something

215

else, alarm. I guessed what they had seen to alarm them. The three men who were struggling over my discarded plastic bag were transfixed in the unexpected illumination. They remained motionless for several long moments before starting to edge their way, cautiously, towards part of the structure that appeared safer.

'Looks as if the fun's over,' I said.

My unwilling companion looked at me sharply. The tone of voice I'd used hadn't been right for a man who had just lost a fortune in diamonds to say nothing of a substantial bundle of cash. 'Fun?' he questioned.

I shrugged. 'Unlike you, I hadn't anything when this little lot started so I'm no worse off.'

'Maybe not,' he said.

'No hard feelings,' I said.

'That depends.'

'On what?'

'On what happens when we get down.'

'What could happen?'

'The police are certain to be there. Someone will have called them while all this was going on.'

'Maybe, but so what? Nobody's done anything illegal.' I gestured over the side. 'All they need say is that they were worried they might be struck up there all night and were trying to get down to the ground.'

He nodded, thinking about it. 'And what will you tell them?'

'I haven't done anything.'

'You've scattered diamonds and pound notes over the crowd.'

I shook my head sadly. 'I doubt anyone saw the diamonds. They'll be gone, trampled into the ground. Maybe the odd one or two might come to light over the years but...'

'What about the money. The crowd won't have missed that.'

'What has it got to do with us? It could've fallen from any of the chairs or it could've come from an aircraft. Anyway, the people who pick it up aren't going to hand it in to the police. Are they?'

'Maybe you're right.'

I could see he still wasn't very happy about everything. 'Look on the bright side,' I said, to take his mind off my part in things. 'These people, the fortune-teller and Jason and their friends must've been causing you a few problems. At least they won't risk getting in your hair again, now you know who they are.'

He seemed to like that. 'No,' he said. 'That's something.'

The Big Wheel began to move again, then stopped as the first chair reached the low point and was emptied. It moved again quickly, the owners were not letting anyone else on until they checked what had gone wrong with the generator. Hopefully Big Eric hadn't done anything too serious. In spasmodic movements

217

we went slowly round. The three men on the framework were off before us. Then Jason. No-one stopped him and he flitted away into the crowd. The fourth man and I were the last off. I glanced round and saw that his partner and the other heavies had been approached by a tall, thin, uniformed policeman who seemed more interested in what was happening a few dozen yards away. I looked in the same direction. It looked like opening day of the January sales and the Rugby League Cup Final all rolled into one, but a whole lot more violent.

Yells and shouts and even a few screams competed with the raucous, musical sounds of the Fair as the unexpected shower of money was fought over. Small wonder the tall, thin, copper wasn't very interested in the climbing activities of the three men. I glanced round and saw Little Sidney and his brothers and wandered over to them.

'See the three men talking to the copper and the one I came off the Wheel with?'

'I see the three, where's the other one?'

I looked round. Bald eagle hadn't hung around to see what happened to his mate. I described him to Little Sidney. 'You'll find him easily enough,' I said hopefully.

'Were they in it together?'

'No, two of them did the job on your house.'

'Which two?'

'I don't know.'

'What...'

'I'm sorry, I thought I'd be able to find out but I didn't.'

'What do we do then?'

'Well,' I said. 'There's only four of them altogether. You don't have to deal with them all at the same time.'

Little Sidney's eyes narrowed and he grinned in anticipation. 'Hear that?' he said to his brothers.

They nodded their heads, all eager to begin.

'Right,' I said. 'It's not my fight so, if you don't mind...' I drifted away from them and worked my way through the crowd.

The last thing I wanted was to get involved in a punch-up. Apart from anything else, I had to collect the real diamonds before anyone found them by accident.

I had reached the end of Walton Street before I felt a tug at my sleeve. It was Big Eric.

He grinned at me and raised his eyebrows.

'Bloody marvellous,' I said. 'Worked like a charm.'

He gave me a thumbs-up sign.

'I'm going off for a few days,' I said. 'I won't be back before the Fair closes. When will you be back in Hull?'

He made a few gestures and I added them up.

'Christmas?'

A nod.

'I'll come and see you then. Tell Aunt Doris

to bake an extra big cake this year.'

He grinned and gave me another upturned thumb. I made the same gesture and he turned and vanished into the crowd, dwarfed by the teenaged giants who towered over him.

I turned and hurried back to my car. I had a few loose ends to tie up before I could take the diamonds and run. As I started up the Cortina I wondered if the bald-headed man would manage to evade the Perkins family.

It occurred to me that, if he did, I might have a loose end that would refuse to be tied up. I pushed the thought out of my mind, looking on the black side wouldn't help, and drove on with the Chuck Mangione Quartet playing *Land of Make Believe* in my ears. I didn't know, at the time, how appropriate that was.

CHAPTER SEVENTEEN

I decided to call into the hospital to see how Carole was progressing, not entirely out of sympathetic interest, but because I thought I might be able to check a few ideas that had been spinning around in my head.

She looked a lot better than the last time I'd seen her. The short period of rest and care had had its effect although, as I sat down beside her bed, I could see a few lines of tension around her mouth and eyes. Being forcibly deprived of both men and booze was starting to get to her.

'Thanks for coming to see me, Johnny,' she said, touching my hand with hers.

'Why wouldn't I?'

'Nobody else has.'

'Nobody else knows you're here,' I said, making light of it.

'There's nobody else to know, not now.'

I frowned slightly, not at the self-pity but at the rider that seemed to suggest her status had changed.

She saw my expression. 'The tattooed man,' she said.

'What about him?'

'He was my uncle. His real name was Charles Dixon.'

So Big Eric had been right about the name. 'I'm sorry,' I said.

'Oh, I hardly knew him. He turned up out of the blue a few weeks ago. Not here, a telephone call, would I go and see him.'

'In Bristol?'

'Yes.'

'What did he want?' I asked, although I'd already worked that out for myself.

'He was very secretive. On the telephone he told me to go to the circus there and wait until he came to me. I did as he asked and when he turned up he had two other people with him, circus performers. He told me later they were

221

acrobats.'

'What did they have to do with it?'

'Nothing. They were there as cover. Neither of them could speak a word of English, they just sat there, smiling and laughing.'

Neat, a nice simple trick to make any watcher think nothing illicit was happening. 'Clever,' I said.

'He told me he had some important business to transact and that he needed my help.'

'Passing packages from him to someone else?'

'Yes. The plan was that he would bring another package. All I had to do was hand his package to the other man and . . .'

'The other man's package to Jenks.'

'Yes.'

'Did he tell you what the packages contained?'

'No. I didn't ask, I didn't want to know, in case . . . in case it was drugs or something like that.'

'You knew it was illegal?'

She nodded. 'It was worth the risk.'

'Worth it?'

'He was paying me fifty pounds every time I made a transfer for him.'

Fifty pounds. Good old Claude, not a man to let a little thing like family loyalties come between him and a fortune. 'How often did this happen?'

'It was supposed to happen every six or seven

weeks.'

'But?'

'I did it once, he gave me a package in Bristol and I made the swap in London on the way back here.' Probably a trial run to see if she did anything dishonest, like opening the package to see if she was being underpaid for her work. 'Then I came back here to wait until he contacted me. He did so last Monday. He said something had gone wrong and he was being watched. He asked me to think of someone we could...' Her voice faltered. 'I'm sorry, Johnny. You were the only one I could think of.'

'That's alright,' I said. 'What are friends for, if you can't use them occasionally. So, apart from the package you exchanged in London the one he left in my car was the first.'

'Yes.'

'So you never made any money out of it at all?'

'Only the first fifty pounds.'

'What about the other man, the one who was supposed to bring you the exchange package. Who was he?'

'I never saw him.'

'But...'

'It was the way he wanted it doing, so I would never know anyone else involved, in case...'

In case she used her information as a lever for more money. I was beginning to like the dead

223

man less and less. I was sure now that the reason he had told her to find someone to use as a temporary post-office wasn't to protect her, it was to protect the chain. He'd been rumbled and he wanted to keep himself and his partners in the clear even if it meant dropping his own niece, to say nothing of an out-of-work steel erector, deep into the mire.

'And you've absolutely no ideas about his partners?'

'No. Unless, unless the two men who . . .'

'No, it wasn't the men who beat you up,' I said. 'They were the opposition.'

'The men who were watching my uncle.'

'Yes, among others.'

'Others?'

'Never mind,' I said. 'It's nothing for you to worry about.' I wasn't all that certain about that. If my guesses were still on the right lines, she might very well have something to worry about.

'Thanks for not being angry, Johnny,' Carole said softly.

I grinned at her. 'Being angry doesn't help anyone.'

'Still . . .'

I stood up to leave. 'Have they said when you can come home?'

She smiled brightly at that. 'Come home. That sounds nice, somehow, permanent.'

I tried not to let the smile fade from my face. I

hadn't meant it the way she seemed to be taking it but I hadn't the heart to tell her. Not then. Later, when she was feeling better, I would make it clear to her that, while I might be a lot closer to needing a permanent relationship than I liked to admit, there was very little doubt left that if I did start up such a relationship it would have to be with someone without her problems. I felt a pang of regret at the thought, not merely at the knowledge that the free and satisfying sexual couplings we'd had were a thing of the past, but that I would miss her in other ways too. Ways I didn't particularly want to investigate too deeply, at least not for the time being. Unfortunately, later on it might be too late, we would be inhabiting different worlds.

I pulled my mind back to the present, hoping that none of my thoughts had shown on my face.

'When?' I asked.

Carole's smile had faded. 'When what?' she asked.

'When will they let you leave,' I said, this time avoiding the use of awkward words.

'Oh, I think . . . perhaps another day or two.'

'Right, I'll pop in tomorrow.'

'Good,' she said, her voice faint and seemingly disinterested. I stood for a moment then said an edgy goodbye and went out of the ward. I resolved to call and see her the next day as I'd said I would. It was the very least that I could do, even though I would be packed and ready to leave town, but I would have to be careful not to let her know it was really goodbye.

I walked down the corridor and thumbed the button for the lift. When the doors opened my informative little nurse was already inside.

'Hello,' she said. 'What brings you here?'

'Visiting a friend.'

'Oh, somebody nice?'

I looked at her and caught a glimmer of something that hadn't been there before. It seemed as if I was being ganged up on by the entire female population. Obviously my passport to a better world had arrived not a moment too soon.

'Yes,' I said.

'Did you find the tattooed man's partners?'

I couldn't remember very clearly what story I had told her. 'Yes, thank you.'

'I saw that pudgy man again,' she said. 'He works here. Does voluntary work.'

'Oh?'

'Yes, he's here tonight. On the tenth floor.'

'Oh.'

The lift stopped and she stepped out. 'Will I see you again?' she asked.

I managed a grin. 'If you say your prayers every night for a week,' I told her.

'I will.'

'Good girl.' I pressed the button for the tenth floor.

'I'll expect you next Sunday then,' she said

and smiled with her tongue on her bottom lip in what she probably thought was a sexy pout.

I smiled weakly and with relief watched the doors close before I was obliged to say anything more.

When the lift eased to a halt on the tenth floor I peered out of it, looking along the corridor both ways, like a fugitive from a second-rate movie. I drifted along the corridor trying to act as if I belonged there.

I didn't see anyone who fitted the nurse's description of pudgy and then a door opened and I was face to face with the worst cornet-player this side of the Pennines. He didn't seem particularly concerned to see me there.

'Why were you asking questions about the tattooed man?' I asked him abruptly while he was still deciding whether or not he was on speaking terms with me.

'Why shouldn't I?'

'Why should you?'

'I can't see what it has to do with you but if you have to know, half the hospital staff went to see him after word got around that he was there. The tattoos were the attraction.'

I could imagine that. 'So?'

'I recognised him of course and naturally enough I asked the nurse who he was, what his name was.'

It didn't sound unreasonable. 'Oh,' I said, feeling slightly ridiculous.

'Why are you interested?'

'No reason,' I said.

'Are you coming to the Haworth again?' he asked. I seemed to have been forgiven my earlier sins.

'I wasn't planning to,' I said.

'It'll be a good night, next Tuesday,' he told me with the air of a man on the brink of revealing something of great importance.

I didn't think next Tuesday could be any worse than the one that had just passed. 'Why?' I asked him.

'Dave Brennan's band is coming over from Rotherham,' he announced.

That was a relief. While Brennan and his boys might not be world-beaters, at least they did quite a lot the regular band couldn't do. For example, they always played in tune.

'Good,' I said.

'They'll have Alton Purnell with them.'

'Will they?'

'I'll see you then,' he said.

'Sure,' I said and walked back to the lift. There wasn't any point in telling him that far from listening to an old New Orleans piano-player in a pub in Hull, I would be on my way to something far more exotic.

As I drove towards B.J. Williams' flat I thought about all the exotic places I would be visiting. The exotic food and drink, the exotic sounds and smells. To say nothing of the exotic women. It crossed my mind more than once that B.J. was somewhat exotic herself, but I pushed that tempting thought aside.

When I rang the door bell I hadn't any particular plan in mind, I would play it by ear. All that mattered was that, somehow, I managed to get into her bedroom.

When she opened the door she looked mildly startled to see me there but she let me in without a doorstep debate.

'Drink?' she asked when we reached the sitting-room.

'Yes please.'

She poured out a generous measure of scotch and I felt childishly pleased that she had remembered what I drank. Then I remembered she hadn't asked me the first time, maybe scotch was all she kept.

'Cheers,' I said.

She sipped at her drink, eyeing me contemplatively.

'You haven't asked me why I'm here,' I said.

'Why are you here?'

'To see you.'

'Are you?' there was a matter-of-factness to her tone that worried me a little

'Yes,' I said. 'I thought I would congratulate you.'

'Oh?'

'Yes. On keeping me guessing.'

'I did, did I?'

'Yes. For quite a time but I caught up with you in the end.'

Her eyes had narrowed slightly. 'You've caught up with me now, have you?'

'Yes.'

'And what exactly does that mean?'

We were having another of our enigmatic conversations. I eyed the bedroom door and wondered fleetingly if the technique that had got me in there the first time would work again. I didn't think it would be but I tried all the same.

'This conversation would be even more interesting if we were in bed,' I said.

She didn't say an immediate yes but, as the song says, she didn't say no. Instead she said, 'Go ahead. I'll be with you in a moment.'

I stared at her thinking that this time she really was making a joke at my expense but her expression didn't seem to say so. I hung onto my glass for support, nodded my head and went into the bedroom. I stood the glass on the bedside table and slipped off my anorak and my leather jacket. Then I went to the door and listened. I could hear her voice, faint and muffled. She was in the kitchen. I looked round and noticed the telephone was missing. She must have plugged it into a jack in the kitchen and was making yet another of her mysterious calls. I was certain this time that I knew who she was calling.

I walked across to the bed, slipped my hand

under the mattress and felt the hardness of the cassette I had hidden there. I took it out and, after a moment's hesitation, slipped it into the top, zipped, pocket of my anorak. Then I sat on the bed and sipped the whisky until B.J. came into the bedroom, closing the door behind her and looking at me with that same odd expression she'd had earlier.

'What did you mean when you said you'd caught up with me?' she asked.

'I know who you really are.'

'Who I. . . what are you talking about?'

'I don't mean your name. I expect you use your real name. Your job, that's what I mean.'

She came closer to me and I reached up and pulled her down onto the bed and held her to me. She didn't resist too much.

'What is my job?' she asked.

'I don't know that I can put a precise name to it, but you and Gostelow are colleagues.' I felt her stiffen against me.

'Gostelow?'

'Don't pretend you don't know the good policeman. That's who you telphoned after you or your partner slugged me over the head the last time I was here.'

'Why would I call Gostelow?'

'Partly to tie me up so I wouldn't get in the way and, perhaps, partly in case I was more damaged than you'd intended.'

'Oh.'

'Well?'

'Well what?'

'Am I right?'

'Maybe,' she said, cautiously.

'Okay, I won't press. I expect you have to keep these things secret.'

'Yes, we do.'

'Customs and Excise,' I said, suddenly.

'What?'

'That's it, isn't it? Customs and Excise, you've been after the diamond smugglers all along.'

I slid one of my hands along her back and began to fumble at the fastening of her dress. I caught a glimpse of my anorak and grinned to myself. A final fling with B.J. Williams then a cassette holder, full of diamonds worth a small fortune, waiting on the sidelines for me to pick up when I left.

Just like a movie.

I had half-removed her dress before she began to respond, her hands fumbled at my trousers and soon she had them loose and sliding down my thighs. Her breasts came into view and I buried my face in them. Then, suddenly, she pushed me hard and I jerked backwards, more in surprise than for any other reason. I glared at her but she wasn't looking at me, her eyes were focussed over my shoulder. I turned round and a man was standing there. I spun round, clutching at my trousers and trying, with difficulty, to keep my dignity.

The man was the actor whose photograph I had seen in the foyer of the theatre. Joe Cornwell. He had to be her partner, I'd already worked that out but I hadn't expected him to be there, witnessing my sexual endeavours.

'What . . .' I started to say.

'Sorry if I'm interrupting anything,' he said, amiably.

'I . . .'

'He knows everything, Joe,' B.J. said.

'Everything?' He didn't seem to like the sound of that.

'He knows we're Customs and Excise officers and that we're working with Gostelow.'

'Well, well.' He stared at me with renewed interest.

'Sorry,' I said.

'Can't be helped,' he said. He glanced around the bedroom and saw my discarded clothes. I managed to fasten myself together and was feeling only slightly less embarrassed than annoyed. B.J. was casually doing up her own clothing and managing to look as if she did that kind of thing all the time. Cornwell crossed to my clothes and picked them up. I tensed but he was merely handing them to me. 'Time we were off,' he said. 'So I'm afraid you'll have to leave.'

I nodded. 'Okay. Don't worry, I won't tell anyone I know who you are.'

'Thank you,' he said, politely.

I turned to B.J. Williams who was standing quietly, calm and detached.

'I'll be seeing you,' she said.

'Probably not,' I said. 'I'm going away for quite a while.'

Everybody makes mistakes and, although I didn't know it, I'd already made plenty but I knew about that one almost as soon as I closed my mouth. B.J.'s eyes widened slightly, then she stepped closer to me and put her arms around me. 'Think about me while you're away,' she said, softly.

I was still thinking about my mistake and the somewhat corny line she just delivered, when I heard a soft footfall on the carpet closer behind me than Cornwell should have been. I tried to turn but B.J.'s arms had pinioned me and I didn't make it before the blow landed.

I watched the carpet rushing up towards me and then, with mixed relief and regret, I dived into it and sank without a murmur.

CHAPTER EIGHTEEN

I tried opening my eyes but everything looked green so I closed them again. I became slowly aware of a tickling sensation along my nose and, cautiously, I opened my eyes once more. The tickling was B.J.'s bedroom carpet and that was causing the green-out as well. I lifted my head an inch and yelped slightly when a sharp pain lanced through it from the point where I'd been hit. I forced myself up onto my knees and examined the carpet in some detail. It wasn't entirely green, it had little yellow flowers in the design. I reached out for the bed and levered myself upright.

'Well done,' a voice said.

I turned round, slowly in case my head fell off, and looked at the bald-headed, eagle-nosed man I'd last seen when we left the Big Wheel. He was sitting by the door, an unlit cigarette in his mouth and, as he didn't appear to be suffering from any damage, I guessed that Big Eric's sons hadn't reached him.

'Did you hit me?' I asked, wondering if my assumption that it had been Joe Cornwell was wrong.

'Me?' he said, feigning innocence that any such thing was likely.

'Why not? You didn't do so badly in the circus tent.'

'Ah. That explains it.'

'Explains what?'

'That three crazy heavy-weights took my partner apart, to say nothing of two of Phillip Jason's cronies.'

Good for the lads I thought. 'It isn't entirely unconnected,' I said.

'Revenge is a sign of immaturity,' he

remarked and took the cigarette out of his mouth and inspected it. He put it back and fumbled in his pockets as if looking for a box of matches. He didn't find one and he stared round and saw my jacket and anorak. He stood up, wandered across and began to look through the pockets. Unsteadily I walked the few paces towards him and casually took them out of his hands.

'I don't smoke,' I told him. I put on the leather jacket and held the anorak loosely in my hands.

He took the cigarette out of his mouth again then replaced it in its packet and went back to his chair, while I resisted the desperate desire to feel if the cassette-holder was still in the top pocket of the anorak.

'What are we going to do about you?' he asked, although it was said in a tone that suggested he didn't expect an answer from me.

'Nothing,' I said and walked to the door. He moved quickly, not far, but just enough so that I couldn't open the bedroom door unless he wanted me to.

'Where do you think you're going?' he asked.

'Out of here, that's all that concerns you.'

'Leave it to me to decide what concerns me, Baxter.'

I looked down at him and some of the irritation at the way my head had been treated during the past few days bubbled closer to the

236

surface.

'Balls,' I said.

'Now, now.' He stood up, his face only inches from mine. 'Go back and sit on the bed, there's a good boy.'

I had hit him before my brain caught up with what I was doing and he slammed back against the door. Irritation or not, my heart couldn't have been in it because he came back at me swiftly, his knee coming up to do more harm than I was prepared to accept. I twisted to one side and the knee dug painfully into my thigh. I dropped the anorak I was still holding and hit him again. This time I did it with all the strength I could muster and my fist went into his stomach with a satisfying thud, followed by an equally satisfying exhalation of breath from his body. I hit him again, this time aiming for the side of his neck. He went over sideways, taking with him the chair he'd been sitting on and a small, delicate, table that looked valuable. He fell on the table and it suddenly wasn't vaulable any more.

He didn't look as if he would be getting up in a hurry and I picked up the anorak and went out, pulling it on as I went. My car was where I'd left it and I climbed in, started the engine and drove away, resisting the urge to check the contents of the cassette-holder until I was locked away where no-one could interrupt.

That somewhere was the public library, in the

reference room where, apart from a couple of bored-looking librarians there were only four or five students earnestly poring over books.

I took out the cassette-holder, it was entitled 'Gems' by Joe Venuti, it had seemed amusing at the time I'd decided to use it as a hiding place for the diamonds, and opened it up. The little wad of cotton-wool was still there. I unfolded it and stared down at the white, fluffy pad. The diamonds had gone.

I sat and stared at the piece of cotton-wool for some time, trying to work out the answer.

When I had said to B.J. and Cornwell that I was going away, I had given them a clue that I might very well have the means for such a journey. That, I was certain, was why I'd been hit again—so they could search me. They would have found the diamonds without any difficulty at all but why would they then go to the trouble of putting the cassette-holder and the cotton-wool back again? It would have been much easier to take the lot. I couldn't imagine they had missed them. Thinking about B.J. again made me wince with the recollection of my assumption that she was on the side of law and order. She must have had a hard time not laughing while she kept me occupied until her partner arrived. I pushed away the thought. It was more important that I worked out where the diamonds had gone. There was always bald eagle. Maybe he'd taken them while I was still

238

unconscious. Perhaps B.J. and Cornwell really had missed them or perhaps bald eagle had arrived before they'd been able to search me and they'd left in a hurry. I felt a sudden chill. Maybe they hadn't left. After I'd knocked him out I hadn't searched the flat, perhaps he'd killed them. I slipped the empty cassette-holder into my pocket and went out to the car and, without thinking too much about it in case I frightened myself off, drove back to Pearson Park and B.J.'s flat. I let myself in, cautiously, and stood in the sitting-room listening. Apart from the sound of my heart, which seemed loud enough to warn anyone that I was there, it was silent.

I opened the bedroom door. Bald eagle had gone, leaving behind only the wreckage of the table to show that anything had happened there. I picked up the chair and stood it by the door. I left the table where it was. Feeling more nervous every moment, I crossed the sitting-room to the kitchen and went in. No-one was there. Then the bathroom. No-one. I was simultaneously relieved and worried. Relieved there were no bodies and worried that I wasn't any closer to finding the diamonds.

I went back out to the car and had just opened the door when a police car materialised out of thin air, the way they do, and stopped alongside me. I recognised one of the occupants from the night in the Hastings' car-park.

'The inspector wants to see you,' he announced.

'Wh ...' He opened the door on the passenger side and slid into the Cortina.

'Let's get moving then. He doesn't like being kept waiting.'

I drove carefully and slowly towards the police station. Carefully, because I didn't want to have an accident when I had a policeman on board and slowly because I was trying to fit Gostelow into things, particularly why he should've sent a car to B.J.'s flat to find me. Whatever his faculties were I didn't think they included second-sight.

This time Gostelow had commandeered a larger office and there were several chairs to choose from when he waved an expansive hand, indicating that I could sit down.

'You've been a busy little boy, haven't you, Johnny? Ah, sorry, Mr. Baxter.' He had a beam on his face that seemed genuine enough. Whatever it was he had in store for me didn't appear to be causing him any discomfort. What it might cause me would, very likely, be a different matter.

'If you say so,' I said.

'Oh, dear me, it isn't me who says so. Far from it. After all, I'm merely a humble policeman. It's other, more exalted beings who say so.'

I couldn't make out his tone. It seemed forced

240

and unnatural but at the same time I was certain he wasn't unhappy about the state of things. 'More exalted beings?' I repeated.

'Yes. It seems you have upset the investigation being carried out by some very important people.'

'Oh,' I said. What was going on? Surely my earlier guess that B.J. and her partner were customs officers had been proved to be hopelessly, laughably, wrong.

Gostelow leaned forward, pressed a button on the desk and sat beaming at me, waiting.

The door opened and I looked up as bald eagle came into the room.

'You've met already, I believe,' Gostelow said.

I stood up, cautiously, not knowing what was going on or what to expect. 'We've met,' I said. The other man's hand went involuntarily to his neck which was discoloured and slightly swollen.

'Yes,' he said quietly, 'we've met.'

I looked at Gostelow and he leaned back in his chair, still beaming. 'Let me introduce you,' he said, with an airy wave of his hand. 'John Baxter, one-time steel erector and failed petty thief, turned diamond-smuggling syndicate wrecker.' The waving arm encompassed bald eagle. 'Joseph Connelly, senior investigator with Her Majesty's Customs and Excise.'

I stared at the other man and he glowered

back at me.

'Nothing to say to one another?' Gostelow said. I finally identified the tone he was using. It didn't take a genius to work out that he was delighted I'd laid out the Customs officer. It explained a lot, Gostelow had been kept off the case because the Customs people were investigating it and they hadn't wanted him around. Nevertheless, as it was all happening on his patch he'd kept a watchful eye on events. That would account for the unlikely fact that he'd had various constables following me around. Not to see that I didn't come to any harm, but to ensure that Gostelow knew what was going on.

'I think we've said it all,' Connelly said, answering the inspector's question.

I nodded my head. 'There's nothing I want to add.'

'Isn't there? Well, if neither of you silent specimens object, there are a couple of things I would like to mention.' He turned to Connelly. 'I would suggest that you take a message back to your superiors and point out that, even if they like to think of themselves as godlike, when it comes down to the nuts and bolts of things, they're no better than the rest of the common herd. Maybe next time they'll co-operate and avoid a monumental cock-up. As for your own part in it,' he gestured at the neck the other man was unconsciously massaging, 'I expect you've learned a lesson or two yourself.'

I grinned at that but then Gostelow turned to me and the beam had gone from his face. 'As for you, Mr. Johnny Baxter. You have a lot of explaining to do.' He glanced at Connelly, and added. 'Explaining that concerns me more than anyone else.'

Connelly took the hint. I had the feeling he didn't particularly want to hang around.

When the door had closed behind him Gostelow turned to look at me again. 'How do you want to do this?' he asked. 'The full thing, the rights, the solicitor, the written statement. Or shall we just have a friendly chat?'

I thought for a moment. As far as I could see, there wasn't anything he could pin on me, unless I told him more than I should and I certainly didn't want a solicitor getting into the act.

'A friendly chat,' I said.

'Good. Let's have a cup of tea to help it along, after all, we might be here for some time.'

We were. It was six hours before he let me go. I told him almost everything. I missed out the fact that the stones I'd thrown into the crowd from the top of the Big Wheel were phony. I let him think they were the real ones. I reasoned that if he caught up with B.J. and Joe Cornwell they wouldn't admit to having the stones, always assuming they had taken them from my pocket.

There was always the chance he would search the fairground and find something. If he did and immediately discovered that all he had was a piece of glass, then he couldn't tie the switch to me. More than likely he would assume someone had been smarter than me. The trouble was, I think he would be right. Someone had been smarter than me, a lot smarter. Needless to say, I didn't tell him about the six thousand pounds. After all that appeared to be all I'd get for my pains. He let me go because, while he could easily have thought up a minor charge or two, that wasn't his style. He wanted someone he could throw the book at, and, fortunately for me, I wasn't the one.

It was approaching seven o'clock when I left the police station and drove wearily back to Park Street. I thought about stopping for some breakfast on the way but I couldn't think of anywhere likely to be open at that time in the morning, apart from transport cafes or the station buffet. As the thought of a grease-laden bacon sandwich from one, or a dried-up cheese roll from the other didn't have a lot of appeal, I went straight home instead.

Someone had been there. Again. This time the search had been even more thorough than before. I sat down in the middle of the mess and started at it all. It must have been B.J. Williams and her friend.

With bald eagle shown to be on the side of law

and order, even if he and his stubby partner had indulged themselves in some rough stuff with me and a few other people, then B.J. and Cornwell must have been Claude Jenks' partners. They wouldn't be amateurs and they couldn't have missed searching the anorak after they'd knocked me out. The fact that they'd come here, to my room, and searched it meant only one thing. They hadn't found the diamonds on me. And that, in turn, meant that the diamonds hadn't been there to start with.

I took out the empty cassette-holder and looked at it, searching for clues. There weren't any. I went through the sequence of events since I'd put the diamonds in there. First I'd put the cassette among all the other cassettes, one among a hundred or more seemed a safe place to hide it. Then I'd taken them all down to Carole's room when I'd thought about leaving town for a few days until things had cooled down. They'd been there when her room had been searched, but judging from subsequent events there didn't seem much likelihood that they'd been found.

After Carole had been attacked I'd taken back the cassette-holder but I hadn't looked to see if the diamonds were still in there. I'd carried it around for a few hours until I got the chance to hide it in B. J. Williams' bed. Then I'd taken it out and moments later I'd been slugged by Cornwell, still without having checked the contents.

It was beginning to look as if the diamonds hadn't been there all the time I'd been carrying the cassette-holder around with me, hiding it and generally endangering my well-being for it.

If I was right the field of people who might have taken them was beginning to narrow. I didn't much like the way my mind was working. I went down onto the next landing and opened Carole's door with my plastic calendar. Her room looked like mine, as if a bomb had hit it. Then I noticed there was something different. In my room the few clothes I owned had been scattered about, here there didn't seem to be all that many clothes. I opened a few drawers and then, with an uneasy feeling growing in me, I searched for a suitcase. I couldn't find one.

I went out onto the landing and dialled the number of the Royal Infirmary. When they answered I asked how she was.

When they told me I hung up, went back into her bedroom and sat on the bed because I didn't want to risk falling over.

She had left the previous evening, about half an hour after I'd visited her. Her departure hadn't been unexpected. She'd been told, earlier in the day, that she would be able to leave at that time. So, when she'd told me she wouldn't be released for a couple of days it had been a lie, a lie that kept her out of my mind.

When the telephone rang I almost decided

against answering it. Then I remembered that the last time it had rung it had been Big Eric with problems. I went out onto the landing and picked it up. The call box signal bleeped in my ear until someone put coins in at the other end.

'Johnny?' It was Carole's voice.

'Hello,' I said, trying to keep my voice natural.

'I'm sorry,' she said.

'Sorry?'

'Sorry I did this to you.'

'I expect you had your reasons.'

'I didn't plan on doing it this way.'

'What changed your mind?'

'You did, at the hospital last night. When I said how nice it sounded, to be going home with you, I saw the look that came into your eyes. You couldn't bear the thought of that could you, Johnny?'

I swallowed. 'That wasn't what I was thinking.'

'I wish I could believe that.'

'You can if you try.'

The telephone began to bleep and she pushed in more coins. 'You were planning on going off on your own, leaving me with nothing, so I couldn't really risk taking you with me. Not when I had a fortune to spend. Could I?'

She sounded as if she wanted convincing otherwise. 'A telephone isn't the best way to talk,' I said. 'Can't we meet?'

'It's too late for that. I'm at Manchester Airport and my flight leaves in less than an hour.'

'I suppose it is.' Her voice sounded faint and far away. 'Goodbye, Johnny.'

'Goodbye, Carole.' I waited until her telephone was clicked back into place and then I ran for the stairs. I had everything I needed packed in less than a minute. Back on the second floor landing a nasty thought hit me and I stopped and dialled a Manchester number and waited impatiently until the hotel I'd booked into answered, then jammed coins into the slot.

'My name's Baxter. I have a room reserved with you and I'm expecting something through the post. Has anything arrived for me?'

'Just one moment sir, I'll check for you,' a slightly nasal voice told me.

I waited, tense.

'Mr. Baxter?'

'Yes.'

'No letters, sir.' Christ, I thought, the bloody post office. 'However, there is a small package.' Heaven bless the post office.

'Thanks,' I said. 'I'll be there in a couple of hours.' I banged the telephone down and took the rest of the stairs two at a time.

I threw the case into the back of the Cortina and headed west. Even allowing for the detour to pick up the six thousand pound package from the hotel, I would be at the airport in less than three hours. Carole's flight would have left less than a couple of hours before I arrived and I wouldn't have much difficulty finding out where she'd gone. I could recall her voice, there had definitely been a note of longing there. She wanted me to know where she was going, that was why she'd told me she was at Manchester Airport and that her flight was due to leave around eight-thirty.

I felt an air of desperation creep into my thinking. I was trying too hard. I was trying to convince myself I wasn't inventing things to suit me. Maybe Carole did think that way but I had to admit there was an equally big possibility that she didn't.

I let my mind wander for a moment to other things, the money at the hotel in Manchester for one. Not a fortune but, by my standards, enough to keep me out of trouble for a while if I took things carefully. I thought about my ex-wife and Susie, who was very nearly my ex-daughter. I would send them something after I'd caught up with Carole, not a lot, just enough to keep the wolf from the door until lover-boy was working. Or maybe it would be just enough to salve my conscience, a troublesome little thought whispered in my ear. And I really would try to come back for Christmas, if only to see Doris and Big Eric and give them some expensive, totally useless gift to show that I was sorry I'd used them. Conscience again I expect.

I thought about Carole. She really had shown far more strength of character than I would have thought possible in someone with her problems. She had hung on, risking and enduring a beating, until I had cleared the way for her to do what I had not dared to do earlier—make a run for it. Perhaps that strength of character meant that she could also lick her other problems, given the opportunity, although I wasn't sure whether or not sudden wealth was a help in things like that or just added more problems. I grinned as I realised I was succeeding in convincing myself that everything was going to wind up with a storybook ending.

Still, there wasn't much point in looking on the gloomy side. Not yet. I selected some music to suit my new-found euphoria and increased my speed as much as the old Cortina would allow.

I was several miles along the M62, floating along to the accompaniment of a joyful, rampaging, version of *Swing That Music* played by Soprano Summit, when an unpleasant thought struck me.

Women can be devious. What if Carole wasn't really at Manchester Airport but had said that to make me chase off in the wrong direction giving herself more time to get clear.

I pushed that thought away, if that was the truth then she need not have called me. I had to be right, but even if I wasn't I still had enough money to last me for a couple of years. That was long enough, amply long enough, to find myself a suitable substitute for Carole Dixon and her fortune in diamonds.

Photoset, Printed and bound in Great Britain by REDWOOD BURN LIMITED Trowbridge Wiltshire